Sons and Fascination

Sons and Fascination

G.S. Mattu

 PaperBooks

Paperbooks Publishing Ltd, 2 London Wall Buildings,
London EC2M 5UU
info@legend-paperbooks.co.uk
www.legendpress.co.uk

British Library Cataloguing in Publication Data available.

ISBN 978-1-9077560-0-9

Set in Times
Printed by Lightning Source, Milton Keynes.

Cover designed by Gudrun Jobst
www.yotedesign.com

'Caelum non animum mutant qui trans mare currunt'
Those who cross the seas change the skies, not their spirits
Horace, Epistles 1.11.27

PART I

1

The train left the station with a moaning intensity, chugging and sparking over the tracks. Jack looked around for an exit sign, people ebbing and flowing. It was sliding towards the evening when he left Embankment station and headed towards his father's club. He walked along the river with the City to his northwest, the breeze whipping across the swollen Thames; the riverside silhouette making postcards at every step.

He took a left turn and walked uphill. He checked he had his keys in his pocket. Jack and his father were supposed to be having something to eat but, most likely, it would be four or five strong Martinis and then the bill. Why they met up, he could hardly tell. Their relationship had always been cool and the passing of time had just made it worse.

His father was just one of the things that had conditioned Jack to always question what it meant to be a man. He wondered what it might be like to have a son of his own. What made it worse was that from the stories that made it past the blockade, from the photos he'd seen and the letters he'd been allowed to read, his father had been so different. There had been a rich, electric talent where now there was a muscular engine; there had been a witty, vivacious man who made people smile and fall in love with him, where now there was a man who wanted to create a distance, who wanted people to fear him, who didn't need the adoration like he once had.

Jack looked at his father across the table in a dim light, sat in comfortable chairs, his lines adding to the handsome mien, the suit impeccably tailored. He felt such little emotion apart from anger, for feeling so little.

"A drink?" his father asked.

"Yes, sure. The usual, I guess."

Alistair beckoned over at a passing waiter, held his arm up at a half-mast, signing 'two' with his fingers, not waiting for acknowledgment. He slid a little into an overstuffed leather armchair. Jack braced himself for the back and forth of conversation.

"It's been tough at work. People are worried, margins are tighter," said Alistair.

"Seems that way, yes," said Jack. "I guess it's not a great time to be planning a new office."

"Well, we had to shelve it for a while. It will still happen, just not – yet." Alistair said this with the displeasure that delay always caused him. "And how do you feel about the question I asked, Jack?"

Jack was supposed to start working in a proposed new office, with a view to eventually heading it up, taking over from a stand-in manager, taking his place in his father's empire of sorts. His father ran a law firm with his old friend, Ray. They had been close since they were at university and had done the stereotypical decadent young professional thing together, finding ways to enjoy themselves around work. Ray's full name was John Raymond Baxbury, which had an air of solidity that Jack liked. Ray was like an uncle to Jack, a warmer proposition than his father, a livelier storyteller, a better drinking buddy. Almost all of what Jack knew about his father's past came from Ray, from a pint or two, a bottle of overpriced red surrounded by pinstripe and loud laughter, from a drinking session after a lengthy meeting. Little bursts of sunlight through an old tarpaulin; soft rain on an eager young face.

The drinks arrived and they sipped, and sipped again.

"I – don't know, Dad."

"You – don't know?" He copied Jack's pause exactly. "What is there that is so hard to work out? This is your family role, Jack."

"It's the family role according to you."

"Whatever it is, this much is true: it is a question that you need to answer soon."

"I thought the plans were shelved?"

"I need to plan ahead. And there are ways to get the money together."

"There aren't ways to guarantee clients."

"Yes, there are. Leave that to me."

For a while, they shared a silence. Across the room came the clink of glasses and heavy 18/8 cutlery on plates. A muted laugh. Jack spotted a couple on a date, the girl laughing for appearances at her companion's anecdote. Fake laughter echoes through the ages. Jack felt the weight of the world, of his fears, of his lack of love press heavily on his temples, the strong cocktail after no food pressing harder than before. Anticipating an Alka-Seltzer at ten in the morning, he thought of long, lonely stretches in a world devoid of comfort; of the gnawing pain of waiting for affection returned; of all of these things, and then he looked at his father. He thought of waiting worriedly at bus stops in the rain, waiting for the big drops to land on the nape of your neck.

"I'll think about it."

A tiny pause. His father looked slightly distracted. "Good."

"Yes, I guess it could be." Jack didn't know why he'd said that. Like about a quarter of all of the things he'd ever said to anyone, he'd struggle to find a reason.

"How is – work?" asked Alistair, seemingly having built Jack's pausing into his repertoire.

"It's fine; I get by. We're working fairly long hours but I make sure I have some fun."

"Are you dating?"

"No, not really. Why do you ask?"

"A man says he's working long hours, it's either to run away from a heartbreak or because you're expecting to run into one."

"In the office?"

"Anywhere. And then you'll be distracted."

"Is that what you call it? A distraction?" Jack felt his face set slightly.

"At your age? Yes, that's what I call it."

"Maybe I'm a little more mature than you give me credit for."

"Jack, I watched you run through girls at a rate of knots at school and tie yourself in knots over some of them. I'm just here to say: it's not worth it." Alistair looked around, nodding at a few familiar faces, smiling at one lady whose laugh tinkled across the room. Making love among the starched white napkins.

"A homograph, now? Very clever. So, it's not worth it, right?"

"No."

"And you and my mother?"

"She was very different to the thin-ice bullshit I see today, Jack. Years go to nothing. Waste comes to waste. We've been through some times."

"And it was just like that: a piece of magic, here you go, a solid lasting life partnership?" Jack ran his fingers through his hair. "Why do you say these things? To piss me off? Or just because?"

"I want you to be spared the pain I know that you're liable to, Jack."

"You do?"

"I do, because I worry about you. You're my only son."

"You – worry – about *me*?" Jack leaned forward.

"I have to say that I don't worry as much as your mother worries – about you in this case – so you might think of me as a mouthpiece. For what we both want to communicate to you. What we want you to *understand*."

"So you actually don't really care either way?"

"You will live and learn, Jack. You have a weak heart. I've seen you fall in love. I want you to fall out of love and into line."

"You're a shit. That's what it is. You love to undermine me."

"There's no need … to use language like that, here. So, if you can't talk nicely, we can just sit here and drink."

Jack said nothing. He sat and he drank. A long while passed. Some jazz was playing very quietly in the background. He watched his father, who was momentarily distracted, before stiffening up slightly. "Sorry to be a pain, Jack, but I have to leave – right now, in fact. Something's come up."

His phone must have gone off in his pocket. Alistair had set it to vibrate differently according to different people sending messages. What was it? A mistress? Ray? A business partner? Jack didn't care. His father motioned again, *two more Martinis*, then got up. Jack still said nothing. He felt something give, like it always did when it went bad yet again, sifting through rubble, throwing mess onto more mess.

"There you go – a head start. Then I assume you'll go out

and do whatever you *do*." Lingering on the last word was his last delay; he headed straight out after shaking his son's hand. Jack sat, his head hurting, wincing a little; two Martinis and the scent of his father's citrus aftershave still in the air. He was such a bastard: in his confidence, his disdain for neediness, and evenings spent like this, wrenching each other with words.

Jack finished his drink, a waiter appearing almost out of nowhere to whisk the empties away. Two more Martinis then and it was only seven in the evening. Where could he go tonight to try and find the elusive One, or maybe the One Right Now, or even just stay alone with the None, drinking at the bar until his legs felt weak and he couldn't feel emptiness anymore. He could head north to Soho. Wend his way to Covent Garden, end up eating a kebab on his knees perched on a wall, somewhere east of the Square Mile, or an empty bus stop 10 yards away, hoping the second night bus of the night would come before daybreak.

The club was well decorated with subtle touches of luxury. The wallpaper was expensive and white with deep red patterning, close to burgundy. It matched the fabric on the chairs around the tables, which gave way at the left of the bar to a set of overstuffed leather armchairs and couches. There were drapes and art on the walls, well-chosen and unobtrusive. A huge print of Rembrandt's *Self Portrait at 63* hung on the right wall.

Jack noticed her first, he was sure of it. Walking through the bank of armchairs and towards the mahogany and polished brass of the bar. She hadn't been there a minute ago.

A girl, a *woman*, looked around the bar, at seemingly nothing in particular. She was stunning, a flow of dark, raven-coloured hair over a pale face, framed beautifully. Her eyes were inquisitive and lively. Jack was given to adoration, given to this kind of impetuousness.

The Martini glass was still frosted. Still angry, he stood up, didn't wait, went over.

"Hello," he said to her.

She turned around, looked closely at him, did a short double-take. He couldn't see any huge significance – just as a sign that she was interested, that he was *worth a second look*. From her eyes, she seemed to be pondering a deep and important question.

"Hi…" she said, about to head into another word, but tailing off, biting it back.

"I've got two drinks, paid for by my errant drinking buddy, who – had to leave," said Jack.

"Right," she said, starting to smile.

"Whoever it is that you're waiting for can wait a little longer while you accept my hospitality, surely?"

There was a pause while both parties tried to get the measure of the other. What did they want? What was the game here, and where was it headed? In the end, the drowsy club, the table waiting, Jack's handsome earnestness – these factors won, and she followed him the short distance to the table.

After they were both seated and she had ordered a cocktail, he tried to find his gear through the fog of a slight headache.

"I'm glad you sat down," he offered, wincing at its lack of artifice, his honesty, so early on.

"Well, you'll find out if you're still glad in a little while, I guess," she said.

"My name, by the way, is Jack." He was suddenly mortified he hadn't done this earlier.

"I'm Francesca. Call me Fran," she said in a beautiful voice, quite vibrant and bright, melodic and sure of itself.

"I will," he said, looking at her directly for the first time, trying to pin some weight behind an eye-contact. The eye-fuck;

he wanted it to topple her by degrees, but she held it steady and led his glance downwards, imperceptibly, with a inclination of her head, a mini-nod down to her chest. He couldn't help but follow and chanced up her stunning cleavage, her blouse just a touch too small, the button closed, but begging to be opened.

"Careful," she said. "I'll have to mark down your scorecard if you look at my chest again." It was only for a second but she'd won that particular point. He looked back up, a little lost, and then she pinned him back, a forceful look backed up with a half-smile and a gentle tilting of her head to the right. He narrowed his eyes just slightly, taking stock. She even picked up on this.

"Not going to throw your toys out of the pram, are you?"

He paused. "No, I was just, wincing from a headache I've had all day."

"Is drinking the solution?"

"I think drinking with you might be *a* solution."

"It doesn't solve anything."

"No. But it creates new problems to take away the old ones."

"I can agree with that."

"That's one thing we can start from then."

"You're not going to start singing Deep Blue Something are you? I don't think I'd like that."

"Um, no." He paused, looking at the thick pile of the carpet. "It's not my thing. I only know the chorus anyway."

"Oh, good." She took a deep sip of her drink, taking it half the way down. He looked at his, fairly untouched. He always felt oddly troubled in situations like this, but the adrenaline from the fear would kick start his conversational skills.

"So, what were you doing at the bar, then, Fran?"

"I was looking for someone."

"And are they yet to turn up?"

"They might do, I've been told I could find them here."

"And they are?"

"It doesn't matter. It wasn't important."

"Well, in that case, can I get you another?"

"You can get me a Daiquiri, yes."

"Sure."

She looked at him and then down at the glass he was holding. "You haven't made much progress on yours. Are you trying to get me drunk?"

"No, I just hate Martinis. It's my father who likes them."

"Your father?"

"He was the errant drinking buddy."

"I see." She paused, looking, then shaking her head just slightly.

"What's the matter?" he said.

"I have an overactive imagination after half a cocktail," she said.

"Well, I'll see if I can deaden it a bit."

"Yes, you do that." She laughed a little and it was a good sound, a sound that wasn't breathy or forced. It sounded natural, at least as much as it could be in the current situation.

Jack looked round for a waiter. He wasn't as good at this as his father. Alistair could always seem to do it with ease, not at all awkwardly, and fit it into the lull in conversation the announcement made. For Jack, however, by the time that the lull was over, there was no waiter in sight. He felt a little sad, as if his failings were being magnified. But he took a chance – he gave her a smile and in doing so let his hand and arm rise up quickly. The blur of white cuff in the air got a waiter to come over to the table.

"Hi," he said.

"What will it be, sir?"

"A Daiquiri, and a… Vodka Mule."

"Excellent," he said as he left.

Jack paused, unsure as to where to take this. He was fairly used to dating girls, to bedding some of them, to having some turn out to not quite like the fragility behind the artifice of his demeanour. He was used to some being hurt by his headstrong ways, too. He was used to trying, to pushing, but not to sitting in a room with a person with whom he was afraid of saying the wrong thing to. This woman in front of him was captivating; the way she was double-guessing him, the way that her hair was tumbling onto her shoulders; the way that she was talking. It was ten minutes in to a random meeting, however, and he couldn't allow these feelings.

These were feelings ruled out by everything he had been conditioned to be; it had to be calculations and pragmatism, a sense of defence. It had to be made New and original and on your terms. He resented a pull into a place he couldn't control. He resented being sent to somewhere he didn't know the layout; he didn't like the feeling that he was sliding down the surface of things.

"What do you do, Fran?" he asked, trying to start it up in a place where he wouldn't have to divulge anything not found on the electoral roll.

"I work in a charity organisation. We help children in the inner cities of England. Um. Before that I did a lot of things: I was a teaching assistant, I worked in retail. That kind of stuff. I'm sure you have a much more elegant story to tell, Jack."

He sensed the trap; why plunge in with the big statement of profession? He was a number like other people, a number that just pulled in more cash for others and got rewarded a little more. At least, that was how the amateur economist in him worked after four pints with his friend Mick; that was the *excuse*.

"I work in law. I've just passed all the exams and stuff quite recently. It's quite modest at the moment."

"Nicely put. I was expecting a bigger ego from someone with a suit like that."

He was forced by the comment to remember how nice his suit actually was, the tailored Hugo Boss lines custom-fit, his shirt double-pleated and the thin grey silk tie.

"It's standard issue. They… give us an allowance."

"They do?"

"No."

"I didn't think so."

"I don't want this to turn into me talking about myself."

"Are you sure, Jack?" She took a big sip of the Daiquiri, again, a quarter of the cocktail gone. Her lips glistened just slightly. He caught a vague green tint in her eyes for a second and then it was gone. Her face was impossibly beautiful and aged into itself, unlike the girls who filled his days and nights. It was starting to hurt to look at her and he wasn't sure why.

"I'm glad I'm not being a bore," he said. He picked up his drink and took a giant gulp, the ginger beer fizzing slightly, the vodka taking the headache away.

He thought about his father having been sat in that chair, his unflinching face, and the way his sculpted features always seem unruffled. This club seemed a ridiculous place to be feeling like that; the club was a bastion of a lack of emotion. It was where people came to rejoice in their status and avoid the crush. Members. *Members* – he thought about it. She must have been signed in by someone.

"So, who signed you in?" he said, regretting it as soon as it was said but, like a text message already sent, it was an irrevocable statement.

"I know the owner. I dated him for a while about a decade ago, when I worked in London."

"I see."

"I moved away."

"He must have been upset."

"He was one of those people that don't really get upset by things like that."

"Oh."

"I think I might be, too." She smiled at him, and he sensed her testing him, wondering what he might say to that. Was he going to say that he too was like that, easy come, and easy go. That he didn't hurt very easily? He did hurt easily. He wasn't entirely sure who he was.

"That's my favourite kind of person."

"You must be very shallow, Jack."

"I'm just unlucky in being drawn to those who'll hurt me. What do they call it?"

"There's a name for the process, I'm sure."

"'The intolerable shirt of flame'?"

"What?"

He couldn't believe he'd quoted Eliot. "It's ... T. S. Eliot. It's from *The Four Quartets*."

"That's quite – that's quite something, Jack. You sure know the smooth lines."

"Yes, I do." He felt very awkward. He took the rest of his drink down and this time caught the waiter's eye. *Two more* he motioned.

There was a little bit of silence.

"Don't feel awkward, Jack. I was just messing with you."

"I guess I might have saved the literati stuff until we were better acquainted."

"Nonsense, lead in with it first off and see what happens."

"And break from the tradition London routine of small talk, large measures and a snog?"

"You should definitely break with that tradition."

The cocktails arrived. "Well, we can start by not having to drink awful draught beer. Here's to my father."

"You're putting it all on his tab, then?"

"He left it open, I think."

"You think?"

"I can get it if not."

"I'd be more comfortable splitting it, considering we've just met."

"I don't think it will be a problem."

Jack didn't usually fiddle. He'd turn the nerves outwards, make better jokes, take off his jacket, roll up his sleeves. However, he was nervous now. He hated his father being right about anything, but there was a truth in some of what he said. It was a vague truth though, a truth without major intuition. He had never known Jack. He had watched and noted, scolded and advised, but he had never made an effort to know his son at all.

Jack turned a corner of the stiff white napkin up and moved his glass a couple of centimetres to the left. "So, is the person you are looking for likely to turn up?"

"It was a speculative mission."

"One of those. I've been on plenty. So I've gone from the hunter to the hunted?"

"Not like that. Someone I knew said I might find them here, but I'm ready to leave after these."

Jack caught the phrase and needed to know what to say. To ask for details or to pre-empt the next course of action.

"We could move on?" She looked at him, and it was a warm look.

"Yeah, let's go after we've finished these." He loved that line. He savoured the sound it made in the air.

2

Jack managed to get all of the drinks on his father's tab. He rather enjoyed the fact that his father would have to pay for them, having basically summoned him, talked condescendingly at him and then headed straight out. Fran had become a little livelier after a few drinks. Her face was animated; the rich beauty took on a life. It was odd to find people who were more attractive when drunk.

She was older than him, but he didn't mind at all. He wondered if she did, if her history would impinge, if she would look at his youthful complexion and laugh. He'd selected a nearby pub so that they wouldn't have to walk too far and he was thankful that they found a corner table. The light was harsher; it did no-one one any favours, but the green of her eyes definitely showed. Her mouth was lined at the corners when she smiled and she had emergent wrinkles at the corners of her eyes. Her porcelain complexion held up; the red lipstick looked even better.

It was a refurbished old pub that had switched its market to after-work professionals. Jack knew a lot of good, authentic places, but he felt that perhaps tonight was not the night for being completely authentic. In fact, he'd never been authentic until it was far too late to care. He'd gone to the bar to get the drinks; he held a lager in a tall, thin pint glass alongside a vodka and lemonade.

They had settled in the table and talked, topics ranging, veering away from how they'd met to more neutral ground. Films and music formed the mainstay; after two more drinks, they allowed literature into the fray. Jack ventured a little more Eliot; she professed that she knew exactly where it was from, that she'd been teasing him.

They kissed at the end of the night. Jack saw kisses as a deal-breaker. He'd heard women see them as handshakes, a way to judge a man, a thing to do before you even come close to making a decision. Take the measure of a man, to test the chemistry, the electricity. Jack decided he didn't want that kind of decision made that night, not this time, not with this woman, and not in his frame of mind. He tailed off the kiss more quickly than he wanted to. He didn't try to push it any further than lips on lips, a slight hip on hip, the mound of her belly pressed onto his belt buckle. She tasted of watermelon lip-gloss.

He took her number; walked her to the Tube; said that he would call her; it was routine, apart from the emotions and the sense of feeling, the stone being stony again, the Underground suddenly rich with colour, the drink suddenly tasting of something apart from numbness it imparted. It was the level of emotion that stops the every day; the feeling that is a world away from moving through the gears, the morning coffee, the first email of the day, the endless blank faces of work colleagues, the small talk in the kitchen, the first customer on the checkout, the first sale in the store. It was a world away from the average dates in average pubs, sealed by sloppy meaningless kisses and broken by unreturned messages. It was a world away from the hard focus on the task at hand and the hard focus on the tasks to come. It was destabilising, ridiculous; it was sublime.

He'd asked her, "do you want to see me again?"

She said that she'd love to.

Jack got home and went straight to his room. He checked his phone – nothing. He resolved not to act too eagerly, not to say, 'are you home?' and to step away from the device. He sat down on his bed, took off his jacket, got up to hang it and then undressed, seemingly in one motion. He left the shirt on the floor, threw his tie on the dresser, and hooked his trousers up on the door. He got to his bed, set the alarm clock, ready for the next day, already swimming out to sea, already sending his thoughts away, looking a face that he could look at for years, missing the last time he felt like that. He was already asking himself if it was the thing that had been absent from his life for the last few years, a time of straightforward sex and poised expressions, of making up to break up, and people always letting go before the undercurrent caught them. He fell asleep, straight away, and he remembered the first time.

3

Two weeks ago, he'd been just off Tottenham Court Road.

"Well, it was a good film, but really I don't know if he cuts it anymore." She paused for breath and took a sip of her Long Island Iced Tea. Rivulets of condensation formed on the glass from there being too much ice in the drink and far too much heat in the bar. "He's always in the news. And the ending was really bad, don't you think? It was all I could do to not just *stand up* and say that this *makes no sense*. What do you think?"

Jack watched her mouth open, and close; open and close. He realised the long beaten-brass bar was sticky and smudgy, but in the dim light it didn't matter so much. They were drinking vertically, leaning on elbows, after a date that consisted of a pack of chewing gum, an oversize carton of buttered popcorn, a film he felt she hadn't understood and now this: a demented Friday crush of bodies and music that was gently stripping his inner ears.

Her name was Susan; that much he knew. Susan from Clapham North, with her plastic bead necklace and thin, toned arms. She had hazel eyes and studiously applied smoky eyeliner. Those features and the rest, he could take or leave. What was it about this girl that made her so tiresome? He sighed.

"I – don't … care?" he said, finally, realising he could walk away, literally *melt away*, into the crowd. And he did, the music drowning out whatever she had to say. He broke the tenuous bonds, spider's silk, and passed through the scrum of bodies with a practised deftness, past the revolving door that served as entrance and exit. He nodded to the bouncer who was too busy anyway, waving underage girls into a world with no exit signs, only doors leading further in.

The street air was cold, but mingled with the muggy warmth of the city at night. A thousand sounds came to him, slowly, as the ringing in his ears subsided. He carried on walking, quickly; took a left, another left; crossed the road as he spotted a gap in traffic and dropped straight into the sludgy atmosphere of the Tube.

It was nine. She'd never call: too proud, too many other options. He wanted something warm and welcoming to take his hand and lead him home.

London is so beautiful at nine o'clock in the evening. Night-vision coincides with the last shades of daylight, which is now fading to the glow of yellow light on dark blue sky – the colours of the night. People walk to and fro; on business, in leisure, not yet drunk, not yet sober, not yet dead.

Tube trains make their arrhythmic click-clack, heading over ground in the suburbs. In the distance the thousand light boxes of a high-rise are like a lattice candle-lamp, the blinking pinnacle of One Canada Square a light house for a city.

Before the date, Jack had been talking to his friend, Gurjit, in a poorly-lit chain coffee-house, that smelled of semi-skimmed milk froth and burnt filter coffee. A quick drink after work and a chance for them to swap stories somewhere quiet, away from the mobs drinking furiously, drinking because it was Friday, and that's just what you do on Fridays.

"Well, if you're taking that angle, there was a lot of beauty around that I missed out on," said Jack, with one eye on the paper. It was around 5.30pm and the café bustled with the tired conversation of workers, drained by dull days, almost recharged by the coming of the night.

"How's that?" asked Gurjit, looking absently into what was left of the foam of his cappuccino.

"I think I was way too caught up in myself, maybe."

"Dude, that's something most of us are guilty of," said Gurjit, looking back at him. "And something that a lot of us never get out the habit of. That's my family *history*."

Now, however, Gurjit had another, makeshift family, which included Jack, his housemate in East London. Dylan and Anne were the other two. Dylan was a struggling writer of sorts, who flitted between jobs, avoiding responsibility, aided and abetted by funding from his parents. Anne was a teacher, slowing getting absorbed into the profession. Sometimes it was all she spoke about, all evening, subconsciously suppressing any risqué language as if she was still in the classroom. *Oh, fudge it*, she's say as her mug toppled off the coffee table. Jack was finishing off his law training and Gurjit was getting into finance.

They all got on, with the usual frictions over who had eaten whose cheese, who had last bought the toilet roll, and they spent dead-eyed Tuesday evenings fighting over the remote.

Dylan had a degree but hadn't yet got a job. Instead, he sat around working on a seldom-seen 'book' that may or may not have existed. Anne would always laugh when he got drunk and, once again, reeled off his 'carrying the burden' speech. But they were laughing together: merry after the third or fourth glass of wine with Dylan climbing on a battered black-leather footstool to make an oration to a forgotten crowd of

Romans about 'talent and responsibility'. Anne liked the role-play about the old London lawyer and the young gentlemen under his wing, a dig at Jack, who would sit and gently uncover his slow-burn smile. She liked it because there was something about Dylan that was a strange blend of Jaggers and Pip, this innocent and zestful bounding and a dark secret; the habitual hand-washer and the twisting London Road to the bright lights and big city.

In the coffee-house, *The Guardian* lay strewn across the table, an artefact from a previous customer, with coffee rings and a small amount of underlining in pencil. Gurjit inwardly winced at what could have prompted this show of erudition. Jack leaned back, rolled a cigarette, deft with his little filter tips.

"Did you read that article in the paper at the weekend, about the low-rise jeans?" Gurjit asked.

"No," Jack said. "Although I can pretty much guess what they were saying. Something about the ironies of the situation, maybe? Prison-wear appropriated for the street?"

"Something like that. I've got it cut out; you can read if you like."

"Life is short enough without cramming it full of bad pseudo-cultural theory, *dude*." He paused. "I have to go meet someone in a little while. A date."

"Well, at least someone's got some action on the horizon. Nothing in ages for me. Maybe I'm going about it the wrong way?" Gurjit smiled and looked at Jack, waiting for some kind of jovial put-down that, oddly, never came. Gurjit with his stocky body, his broad, handsome face, black Armani jeans.

"Just keep on at it, Gurj. It's the only way. See you."

Jack got up, shook hands with Gurjit. He'd not done this at the start of their friendship, but Gurjit had insisted, his

Punjabi roots, a male camaraderie built around handshakes, big drinking and a forced suppression of feelings.

"Laterz," he said, hanging on the 'z', letting his handshake linger.

Anne was across town, eating. She's eating a Caesar salad, drinking a medium bottle of sparkling water, sitting. She sits opposite a teacher friend, who is taking apart a club sandwich. She thinks – maybe – that she likes him. Her brown, shoulder length hair, which curls a little at the ends; her oval, deep brown eyes; her lilting, girlish voice that soothes. She gently picks at the salad, watching her weight, watching what she says. Words stumble on her mental tripwire, enmeshed in eddies, currents and whirlpools beneath the surface. The café they were in was busy, a waitress bustling past to deliver to plates of food, heaped with chips. The teacher friend leaned in.

"Do you like your salad?" he asked.

"I'm not sure," she said, smiling. "I need to think about it a little more."

Anne was pensive. All of her housemates had been struck at her quiet moods, sitting in the corner of the armchair with a glass of wine on the coffee table beside her, slowly and methodically making her way through a magazine. She would look up at Jack, and look down again. He caught her, a few times, her gaze unsure, her top teeth biting into her bottom lip. It was as if she wasn't sure what she wanted to learn. The television would drone on and Dylan would pass out after two joints, head back and to one side. Anne was weak spring sun filtering through surface ice. She'd moved in with everything packed neatly in clear plastic crates with lids on them. One by one, the devices: a DeLonghi filter machine, a food processor. Joni Mitchell albums stacked up in her room amongst Kirby grips and the awful anticipation of vulnerability. Sometimes the four housemates would all wear their big coats and pace around London in a gang, Jack smoking, Gurjit with his bulky arm linked with Anne's; Dylan would hold forth vaguely about something or other until he would grow silent; and they would fill with the awe of what London is. What the city could do, what this place was not.

London is not beautiful, and people are fed lies like they are fed additives and colorants, preservatives and refined starches, culture and attitude, aspirations and aspirin, to cure the hangovers of aspiration's death.

The station at Mile End, with the puddles between the tracks, chocolate wrappers slowly returning to the pulp from which they came, lying close to the remnants of cheap snacks and commuter food. The junk to keep passengers going as they rock in their steel-carriage travel-amnesia, back home to eat, watch some television, think about a drink or two then go to bed. Someone writing to their lover, someone sitting on a chair in tears. Dylan wakes up at six-thirty in the evening, intensely hungover. There is a bottle of red wine beside his bed, empty, lying on its side. *What have I done with this year?*

Outside in the September sky the darkness is slowly forming out of what is left of the light of the day, and soon the night will become a grey, tinged with red.

This is what characters in London stories do: they might read the *Evening Standard*, buy a tube ticket and go to Camden to score something. This particular Londoner slowly gets out of bed, sighing as he rises. It is a practised routine, it accumulates like limescale; an arteriosclerosis of the pulsing lifeblood. Dylan puts down his pen and can't write anymore. Jack returns home from work and can't remember a thing he did that day. Feeling like that, a drink and the television might make an evening pass. Dylan is already on the couch.

Jack hangs up his black jacket and loosens his tie, turns on the kettle, finds his mug. He could travel to the ends of the earth and the thought would remain, like memories of sparking snatched kisses in a neon blur, exam papers and ink-stained fingers. Now, the dullness of those same fingers on keys as the years tick by on a metronome. He was here, this was him; those who run across the sea change the sky, not their spirit. From his father, engraved on a pen, but at the same time the summer was starting, exams receding, Parker ink flicked over a whitewash wall in a splatter as someone called a dealer and someone got the drinks and he called his girlfriend, dropping the phone in a pint of London Pride. He'd bent the nib that year; twisted metal like a spider's calligraphy.

He sat down and waited for the news to come on as Dylan fell asleep on his shoulder.

4

Earlier that day it had been raining again, pattering heavily on the windowpanes.

Jack was downstairs, waiting for the stovetop coffee-maker to bubble through its motions. A solitary slice of toast popped out of the silver Dualit that Anne had brought to the house. He spread some margarine, perfunctorily, took a bite, and returned to the delicate act of adding just enough sugar and just enough milk to his finished coffee. It was a morning ritual that he relied on to take his mind off the pile of dishes in the sink and the rain outside. The Tube would be grotty and damp, waiting like it knew he was coming, knew he could never get away.

He put the milk back into the fridge and noticed someone had taken a big ladleful out of the pasta bake he was planning to eat that night. A bitter rage flared, followed just as quickly by a feeling of resignation. He wasn't going to have it any-way – he had his date with Susan, who he'd met at a house party where the most interesting thing was how many people had managed to get into the kitchen at one time. A man with some indefinable but grating accent was making bad jokes and someone was beseeching everyone to play drinking games in the equally busy living room.

He'd gone out to have a cigarette and there she was, looking oddly frail as she took a drag on a Camel Light, with what looked like a tear in her eye. He'd been perfunctory: are you alright, I have to go, *here's my number*. Her eyes were bloodshot; she'd not remember much. He hurried back to the bad-joke man in order to take him to one side and explain that his friend, whose party it was, was deeply offended by his racial and political humour; that he'd called a mutual friend, Gurjit, who was en route to forcibly expel him from the house. The man had backed up, grinning; *who's Gurjip, then*? He found out, after losing a tooth that night.

Jack slammed the door on the way out; it seemed fitting.

Dylan was making love to the librarian's daughter in his room. It was hot and they were lain on their sides. He was behind her, taking her vigorously, feeling her rear-end against his lower stomach, noting a sense of fulfilment and purpose move up from his groin in a circular radius. He pictured concentric circles of primary colours.

They had met through the bookshop. During an idle conversation at the till, the librarian herself had let slip that her daughter worked weekends there. She was called Lauren and wore titty-jumpers and thick rimmed black glasses, perfumes with notes of vanilla. Her smile made him think of something healthy and alive.

Before the sex to his then-coy mistress, Dylan had promised that unless she went to bed with him, worms would try her long preserved chastity. *Marvellous*, she'd said, and he'd laughed, loving the wordplay. He liked so much about her, so what was it that held him back? His father, who modulated down to him, in imperious tones, the sedimentary accumulation of some supposed familial wisdom? A boy and man knocking off the hours with a fishing rod in the damp February afternoons; *don't get too close, my boy*. A flick of the rod, a grin as wide as the river itself; *I've got one!*

You're sure did, Dad, Dylan noted, absent-mindedly kissing the back of Lauren's neck. *But she hates you more than you know.*

He came – pleasure-wave, numb-phase, guilt-wave – a familiar scenario. Lauren bucked, on the verge, his fingers upping their efforts, her back arching slightly, her front teeth digging into his arm, which lay underneath her hair-matted head. There was a healthy sheen of perspiration on them both, and Lauren pushed back, her beautiful rear-end fitting snugly into him. He withdrew, took off the condom, feeling oddly nauseated by the return to the mundane.

Lauren smelt of life, of love, and a future that was cast out of terracotta clay, decked with fresh-cut flowers; not the grey, chrome-tinged melee that London promised, day in, day out. She nuzzled back a little more and they fell asleep. Sex: breakfast of champions. Dylan's mind fuzzed up with a knowledge that something this good and right could never last.

5

As the week progressed, it was getting a little warmer. The clouds would part and London would see some sunshine at low angles, dazzling drivers on the wet roads. It hinted at Spring, when the flowers would grow and everything would be *bathed in sweet liquor*. Anne would roll around drunk and fucked on Pimms and lemonade, perverting Chaucer as she went. With her tartan throws in a green London park, the rangy grass would show signs of new life. It was sunny when she got up and, upon leaving the house, the slanted light warmed her head.

Work started well; the first class went well. To her surprise, she had got on famously with the cover teacher she had wanted to ask for lunch; to her surprise he actually asked her. She was further surprised when he asked her again after-wards, for a coffee or a drink.

They had sat in a bar with a glass of Pinot Grigio for her and a pint of Amstel for him, the drinks placed on napkins as he paid. He brought them across, sat down, and she thought that he walked like Jack. He had stubble, too. She sipped her wine and smiled at him.

"Is it okay?" he asked.

"It's nice," she replied. She said more with her eyes, inquisitive and locked onto his. She was wearing a white blouse and a v-neck jumper over it. He had a jacket over a blue shirt. He looked down at the table, his finger tracing a little shape, and as he looked up, her eyes were still on him. Anne deliberated in moments like this; luxuriating in the subtexts. She hardly knew that she did it. Time passed and the pause stretched. They both knew that one, or the other, had to say something soon.

"Have you seen that film," she asked. "The one that's all over the papers?"

"The one with the *ending*?"

She laughed. "Yes! The one with the *ending*. You know what, I watched it and I can't even remember what it was called."

"I think it was called *The Ending* … honestly." She was grinning and he was almost put off by how feline her pose was, curves and shapes. "That's the one that you're talking about, right?" She nodded. He carried on. "What did you think of it?" he asked.

"Do you know what … I'm not sure what I thought of it. I wasn't sure even right after I'd seen it."

"I saw it with a friend a couple of weeks back," he said. He was careful not to weight the word in either direction. "I think he's pretty overexposed, that's the problem. There's no surprise to anything. And he plays the same part so often."

"Well, they're the ones always banging on about him, hiring him to do it, too, what do they expect?" She paused. "They can't turn around and say that it wasn't their fault, at least to some extent." She took a larger sip of wine and smiled slightly.

"I always find talking about the cinema a bit difficult," she said.

"We could talk about the Year 10s if you want?" he said,

bringing the pint up for a sip, which turned into him taking a third of the pint She winced a little as she glanced back to her own glass of wine with its presage of a slow getting to know you. "Some of those kids. Unbelievable. One of the little bastards tried to throw his shoe at me. His *shoe!*"

She let her mind drift away as he slowly talked and drank his way out of her address book.

Meanwhile, across town, a man called John Raymond Baxbury remembered at the instant before they injected the anaesthetic that it was *he* that had stupidly initiated the festivities – it was he that has asked his now-wife to marry him. That day in the restaurant seemed decades ago – it *was* decades ago – but it was like a sepia-tinted photograph with two beautiful strangers who were very much in love. He looked mildly bemused as the doctor explained to him how 'doped up to the back teeth' probably got its name.

"It's because, Mr. Baxbury, when you have your back teeth out, as you are having done now, you really need these anaesthetics."

He then veered onto a banal topic, perhaps the weather. John felt oddly insecure. How long had it been since he'd gotten his hair cut? Was the shower still broken at home, spraying its little spurts of water past the safety of the shower curtain and onto the carpeted bathroom floor?

"Now, we'll just count to ten," the dentist informed him.

"One, two –"

Sleep comes like a drug –

His wife was back in the waiting room but had spent the consultation session mildly flirting with the dentist, presumably to wind him up. And it worked as John was tempted to find out how good his tooth repair skills really were. It was decades since he'd memorably ratcheted Alistair Wilson, a partner at his firm, in the middle of the office after a boozy and distinctly acrimonious lunch.

"Mother?" he asked, before he nodded off.

Anne was no mother. She was a temptress since her French revolution on the Modern Foreign Language degree, had been there in the 1700s in her history class, calling for their heads and hearing them sing for freedom. It was the best of times, it was the worst of times, but to be young was pure – bliss? Her Dickens wasn't any better than her faded memory of *The Prelude*, an asexual Wordsworth walking away from a woman, Dickens loving the mirrors in his room.

Her parents told her that university would solve her issues. They didn't, however, tell her to watch out for the sudden moment when the final term ends and the resolution so long desired is either forced upon you or forcibly gone. Now this was her university, this bleakly furnished school with her rabble of rough-housing children eating soggy fries at lunchtime. She longed to get home, to uncork a bottle of Blossom Hill and feel that *warmth* again.

Jack was home early, tired, and he felt dismal; he was broken by the incessant rain. He looked at the Blossom Hill bottle as he surveyed what was in the fridge. He called Mickey, a friend of his who'd have some good weed. Mickey lived not far away, in a studio flat not much bigger than the living room of the red-brick semi that Jack stayed in. He insisted on his own space, viewed it as a base to build on, and rarely wanted to take girls back there. He came round with the requisites and, as Jack opened the door, Mickey was there with a bright, sunny smile that belied the evening's gloom.

"Michael Farringdon, nice to see you, sir." Jack shook his hand, surprised that it was dry. The grip was firm and Mickey wasted no time in hanging his coat and taking a six-pack of imported lager to the kitchen. He looked around, and shook his head. "Do your dishes, man, this is a shit-hole."

"Just make a space on the worktop and roll a joint, you tool. Do I complain about the boxer shorts strewn round your pokey little flat?"

"I suspect, from the fact you don't, that you rather like it like that. Reminds you of all the young strapping men that have passed through your life?"

He let that one go by. Jack opened the fridge, put the beers in, felt the cool air against his face. "Pizza?"

He got it out, displayed it to the at-work Mickey on his right.

"Yes… but put some more cheese on the stingy fucking thing; where'd you *get* that?"

"From the supermarket."

"The fucking bin, more like, why the fuck is it so floppy?"

"It's not cooked yet!"

"More cheese. And some of those crushed chilli seeds. And then boot up the console."

"Anything else?" asked Jack, exasperated but smiling, slowly.

"Is Anne going to be around tonight?" Mickey had a crush of sorts on the entirely incompatible Anne.

"She did actually send me a text." Jack thought for a moment. "She was on a date with some drippy colleague."

"Can I have the *number* yet? The infamous *number*."

"No. Ask her yourself."

"Now who's the tool, Jack?"

"I've seen the filthy shit that you send when drunk, Mick, and I can barely see it working even on the skanks you pull."

"Pizza and PlayStation, and then we'll talk in more detail about said skanks," said Mickey.

He was back at work on the joint, turning over, behind a shock of spiky ginger hair, exactly how he'd have sex with Anne. He concentrated and let the hum of the kitchen subside, let the sounds of Jack working on the pizza fade back until all he could hear was Anne moaning something into his left ear as he nuzzled hers, the world turned upside down.

Jack's world was unstable. There was an accumulated debt of the sins of the father that the son was about to stumble into. As Jack combed his hair in the morning and felt that gentle sway from too much weed the night before. He wasn't ready to meet a woman called Francesca, and wasn't prepared for all the things that would ensue from meeting a glance, offering attention and having that glance and attention reciprocated. Words build upon words, actions upon actions.

6

Every free flowing action for Jack was imbued with a sense of come down, a breaking down into the details. It wasn't that he thought of consequences; they were often ignored altogether. The actions however were quantified; they were stretched out on a table and examined for their quality.

Mickey was again round his place and they were sitting in the living room. A few beers, a games console and some television. Mickey was crumbling some weed onto a magazine, one of Anne's, with Jack on the couch next to him. Anne would often fly into as much of a rage as she was capable of when finding bits of weed in her *Vogue* or *Cosmopolitan*.

"This is... unacceptable! Jack!" she'd say, staccato and wide-eyed.

Gurjit was sitting in the armchair, just across the room, humming a tune gently and knocking his way through a bottle of Bacardi. He only had to change the ice every three drinks because of the rate he was going through it. Some bhangra came from his earphones, just the beat and the occasional sarangi riff biting across the treble. The TV was tuned to BBC2, turned low, the talking heads looking slightly manic as the stereo easily overpowered them. They were listening to a radio show that was mostly playing electro-rock. Depeche Mode's 'In Your Room' was on.

"Turn the lights up, man. I can't fucking see what I'm doing," said Mickey, overemphasising a fumbling action.

"I'm trying to keep the mood. Anyway, Gurj says he has a headache."

"Oh he does, does he? *Stop drinking so much fucking rum*, then, *dude*. That might help?" shouted Mickey.

Gurjit mumbled a response and carried on listening to whatever was piping into his ears.

Jack open two more cans of beer and poured them into tall glasses. As he did, carefully, deliberately, Mickey took the chance to open up the floor.

"You wanted to talk about this bitch, right?"

"Mick – she's not a *bitch*. What is your problem with terminology?"

"Right, girlfriend, woman, whatever. So – you met her when?"

"Last night."

"Last night? And you already need 'advice'? Are you turning into something out of a broadsheet lifestyle column?"

"Look, be serious."

Mickey turned to take stock of his friend. Their eyes met; Jack looked earnest, if a little vulnerable behind the usual maintained stubble and the half-smile. He kept smiling as Mickey put down the block of weed and turned even further towards him. The smile flickered just for a second. Mickey knew this man well, knew that flicker across a table in a pub, across a dance floor; he knew what the flicker meant and the turn of events that might engender it.

"Tell me, then. Tell me while I finish skinning this monolithic bad boy up. This... this is a work of art." He started grinning.

"Okay, well – I met her last night at Dad's club; she was there just hanging around it seemed. Apparently used to date the owner, so I guess she 's been there a lot. I invited her over, we had some drinks, and then some drinks turned into more drinks, and at the end of the night we kissed."

"So far, so good, sure. But what's the reason for the special measures?"

"What special measures?"

"Don't kid me, Jack."

"What are you talking about?"

"You think, after watching you chase tail for years, I don't know when you actually bite on a hook from someone up the food chain?"

"That's not fair."

"It's the truth, man. I can read you. Just like you can read me. Look at me, what am I thinking?" Jack looked into Mickey's blue, unwavering eyes.

"You are thinking, 'I would quite like to smoke this joint now'."

"See how easy it is, man? You are damn right. Now, pass that fucking lighter over there and keep talking."

Jack tossed it across and carried on while Mickey set about bringing his apparent cigar of a joint to life. "She was very cute, yes. Older, and still really beautiful, but mature with it, and funny, and it didn't feel boring; it felt quite different. It felt new."

"A new Oyster card holder feels new, Jack. A new pair of boxer shorts can feel new. Older, huh? So, how old? Old enough to not be 'quite new'? Fifty? Are you going to bang a coffin dodger now and call it a sport?"

"Mickey, stop it man. It's not funny."

"You would have laughed last night if she'd said it."

"She's hardly likely to call herself a coffin dodger, you fuck. She's like, forty or something."

"Dude, she's nearly twice your age! London is rammed

with girls who want to sleep with you, Jack. You're good looking. You practice law. You're a catch. Take this," said Mickey.

Jack took a hit, while Mickey decided to seek out some more detail. "So, you met her last night, you feel a bit weird, and you wanted to ask me about it?"

"No, I wanted to get high. It's a good chance to ask your opinion, though?"

"My opinion counts for shit, man. I don't think I've ever loved anything except my parents and a choice few of my gadgets. Much easier that way – less potential for acrimonious heartache and much more potential for fuck buddies."

"You're going to grow up to be the worst person in East London, Mickey."

"Well, if you turn into your Dad, we'll have a great laugh together. And your wife will be ninety so she won't care when you come home, either. "

"Nice." There was a pause.

"Where's that hot piece of ass Anne?"

"She is out. On another *date*."

Mickey took a big gulp of beer and took the joint from Jack. It was strong stuff and they felt it come on quickly. The Depeche Mode track finished; 'Your Silent Face' by New Order replaced it. "She needs me to lay it on her man. Forget her co-workers and that 'friendship group'. They're all idiots."

"They are inoffensive and non-threatening, and that's what she likes about them, Mick. You would literally cause her to shrivel up."

"I think I'd probably have the opposite effect, if you follow."

"I could follow, I just don't want to get to where you're going."

"Missing out, man."

"I am in a predicament of my own."

Mick passed the joint back. "You are? Aren't you going on another date?"

"She might very well be too old, dude. She might think I'm too young. It might be awkward."

"And these things have bothered you since when?"

"Since I can't concentrate at work?"

"That's a problem you share with the entire office-based world, man. We're all just looking for ways to waste our time."

"I mean, I really can't concentrate. Even on slacking off. It hasn't happened for a long time."

"So, you feel – what?"

"This is going to sound stupid."

"Again, not that much of a surprise, but go on."

"I feel – teenage. Like I did with, well, you know who."

"Oh man, why would you bring up that shit-bag?"

"I'm not talking about the end of my time with her; I'm talking about the start."

"Every end is related to the start. It's the same thing. Stay away from that shit. It can only end in badness, Jack."

"Only?"

"Every single *mo'fucking* time. You name a time when you had that prescient feeling along with the weird lack of focus, and you will find a car crash and a man all tangled up in it, moaning to his friends and being a miserable bastard."

"That's really pessimistic."

"Life is cruel."

"What about Sally?"

"She wasn't worth it."

"In hindsight?"

"Even then; it wasn't worth the pain of anticipation. It

wasn't worth the green-eyed monster fucking with my head. It wasn't worth her cheating on me, either. So no, Jack, it wasn't worth it, and if you're hooking your keys on some old broad who probably has form, then you know that I *told* you, okay?"

"Yes, you told me."

Mickey stopped and let the joint burn down. He got melancholic whenever Sally came up. For brief flashes; only for seconds at a time. His guard was up forever, probably – that's what Jack guessed. Mickey had dated her at university. He had dated her and he hadn't quite been the same since.

"Gurj," said Mickey. He didn't hear, still with his eyes shut and a drink in his hands. "Gurjit!" Mickey shouted and got up. He had to reach into him and take one of his earphones out. Gurjit roused himself back around.

"What are you doing? I'm having a lonely night in. Why are you making this difficult?"

"Can we set up some shots, dude? Just to catch a bit of a buzz."

"There's a bottle of Grey Goose under the stairs, man. Ice is in the freezer."

"Cheers."

"No problems. Can I – tune back in now?"

"Yeah, have fun."

"Ha. Fun." He put his earphone back in. Jack looked at Mickey. "He said he was missing his dog, but I don't think that's the reason, to be honest."

"We all miss something, or something misses us. You know," said Mickey, as he headed to the cupboard under the stairs with new purpose. Jack lit the joint lying in the ashtray and leaned into the soft leather couch, missing something quite keenly. He'd not figured out what. He'd been asking the question since he was fourteen-years-old.

7

Dylan sat across from his girlfriend and asked if she would like to go away with him. He'd always wanted to go on a city break to Barcelona, and his Dad had just sent him some cash as apparently 'business *was* good.' Business was good, if it sent him on free city breaks to exotic locations.

They were in a café with scratched formica tables which seemed to be stood in time apart from the fact it served Thai food alongside fry-ups. Builders with big hands ate Thai Green curry; a giant contraption for providing hot water stood at the counter, piping steam into the air.

"I can't Dylan."

Dylan prepared himself for the argument; she was too busy, couldn't get the time off. It was a library; they'd manage. He opened his mouth to say this when she added, "I can't do this."

He stopped dead in his tracks and felt a wave of nausea hit him. The old lie, that it would work out, had worked on him. It wasn't going to work out. He'd heard it before, 'I can't do this,' always in tones that rose when there was ground to make up, a relationship to save. She had said it flat, almost falling at the end into the full stop.

"I can't do this," she'd said, and rather than enter the world of pain that ended in recriminations and blame, in resentment and futile gestures of amicability, 'yes we can friends, of course I want to spend time with you, you're a great person', he stood up and walked out, and didn't stop moving once until he was all packed for Barcelona.

Jack wasn't too far away, walking across Waterloo Bridge on his way to Holborn. He looked across to scan the river. He felt a little nervous on his way to meet Francesca for their second date. It was the 'difficult second date': the one where you can't rely on the initial burst of information, where everything is new, where the common ground scenarios arrive or are forever delayed. He'd called her; he didn't want to send a text message. She'd picked up on the fourth ring, sounding jovial and pleased to hear from him.

So here they were: meeting in a pub in Holborn, maybe en route to get something to eat. London is an endless world of possibilities when the outlook is good and you feel energetic. The pavements and the side-roads, the cafes and the public houses, home to the stories of the city and the millions who live in them, basic narratives in a cumulative deluge of plot. The stage for the millions who work, who play, who go back and forth across tried and tested routes.

Jack felt better than he had done the day before. There was a little less of that odd pain of unknowing mixed with the pang of desire. Even a few days make all the difference; from the kiss to the timing being wrong, the paths aren't aligned, we aren't headed in the same direction. It's not quite right. He'd taken his acute ache from a few nights before and turned it into something that was close to manageable. Put those things in a box and shut the lid. It was the dull ache of a happening that could be good, could be amazing, but was beset by odds from all sides. It was the pragmatism not the idealism that governed the day-to-day and made you turn away from caressing a face on the train, or leaning into a stranger and asking if they had plans, that night, or the next night.

He'd left work a little early; it was still light when they met although the sunset was fast casting long shadows and bringing in a cold breeze. He spotted her quickly, dark hair in the corner, looking down at a phone and then returning to a glass of what looked like water. He went up to her, casually, as slowly as he could manage so as to avoid the startled hello that could strangulate a first exchange.

"Um, hi, Fran," he said, as she caught his blazer in her gaze and looked up. She smiled at him, putting her phone into her pocket.

"Hi Jack. Just in time, I've managed to get to the end of my lime and soda. Perhaps a glass of Rioja might fix this sadness?"

He liked the relaxed start and took the hint, heading straight to the bar. She knew what she wanted out of conversational exchanges and that much he genuinely appreciated. The bar was busy; he waited until he got a chance to put an elbow down on it. He looked up the barmaid: petite, lively and cute. He made some eye contact and then led with his eyes to the taps; she got the message and responded to the lack of overture. She came over and asked in a surprisingly husky voice what he wanted.

"A Kronenburg and a… large Rioja, please."

"Sure thing, love."

"Great."

She went to get the wine, on a lower shelf, and bent over very deliberately, ensuring Jack had a view of her well-proportioned rear. She was wearing low-rise jeans with French knickers, and above that was a patch of her back, bordered by two dimples. Her top was black with a fine gold mesh somehow resting on it. The barmaid popped up with the bottle, took a wine glass and a pint from the shelf, pouring the wine whilst flipping the lager tap up. The hubbub of the bar filled the space between them. As she turned, punters jostled to get her attention. Someone at the far end was waving a ten-pound note frantically, obviously to her irritation.

"Nine-fifty, please."

He handed over a tenner.

"Not very talkative today?"

"I'm – well, I think the lady is waiting for her drinks." Jack beckoned over to Fran.

"Of course she is. Well, you have fun," she said, and immediately turned her head to serve whoever was next.

Jack took the drinks, sipping a little of the pint to avoid spilling it on his way back. He sat down with a sigh, and started to talk about his day.

"The office was quite manic – "

"Do you know her, Jack?"

"The barmaid? No, I don't."

"Oh. She obviously took a liking to you."

"What can I say? Maybe she liked the blazer?"

"Very cute, yes. I can see you're no stranger to attention."

"She wasn't really my type."

"Well, now, that's a bold statement. What *is* your type, Jack?"

He hadn't planned that particularly well. Resting his lips on the pint to take the head down, he ran his tongue over his top lip at the point under his nose. Finally, he laughed.

"Two minutes in and I'm floundering?"

"Two minutes and you just aren't *playing the game*, Jack."

"What game is it?"

"We've surely got to make this as difficult as we can before we admit that we quite like each other?"

He paused. He saw the strategies, the role she wanted him to play.

"Yes, let's make it difficult." He grinned his easy grin, taking his pint in his right hand and lifting it up. "We didn't toast to our date."

"I was making it difficult. You still want to toast?"

"I'm happy just to carry on, I think."

They carried on, and one drink became two, and three. The light shifted in the pub as the sun set fully and night came in. They moved to a bar that Jack knew nearby, where there was the kind of jukebox that spurred you to worry about those important albums you'd never bought. The tables were rough and slightly worn and the art on the wall was for sale, but Fran seemed to like it. They got closer; kissed each other. Fran's smell made Jack giddy. The leather of the couch and her perfume, her clothes and expensive shampoo; it all came together. The wax in the candle that was set into a bottle of Jack Daniels, the sticky patch under the left forward leg of the table where someone had spilt some wine earlier.

They came together. What had happened to his poise that made him think of giddy kisses in bars as a teenager, tasting lip-gloss like it was crack, drinking in the time spent and anticipation of time spent to come, as if it would fill up the void? It all came together.

Fran's apartment was on the ground floor, about half-an-hour out from the centre. It was sparsely furnished, with a deep red couch and laminate flooring put in by the landlord. He asked her, when they got there and had finished kissing, if this was her idea. She said, "What this?" and he said "No, the couch". She laughed and after that it was just touch and taste and pressure. He sat her down on one of the arms of the armchair in the living room and bent down to kiss her and take her head in his hands and for once he didn't feel like he was running through the motions and that in itself was a beautiful thing and he felt someone grab his back and it was Fran –

8

Jack met John Raymond Baxbury in a scuffed London pub at seven, finding Uncle Ray at a table, sat on a stool, halfway through a Guinness and some potato wedges. He lifted his head as Jack appeared and put out a hand, Ray's handshake firm and steady. Ray was stocky and well-set, his face a square kind of handsome, lined with age and some hectic living. His eyes had dulled with the passing of time and marriage, the rows and recriminations of childlessness and the slow death of affection. He stood up to get Jack a drink, and Jack waved him down. Status Quo were on the stereo.

"I'll get these. Guinness?" said Jack.

"Yes, please."

"Be right back." Jack set off to the bar with a practised rhythm and timing. He got served quickly and came back with a little bit of beer on his fingers, which he gently wiped off into a napkin that Ray hadn't used. He took a sip, then offered Ray a cheers. Glasses clinked and then he sat back, exhaling slowly.

"So, you wanted to talk about something then, Jack?"

"Yeah, I did. We'll come to it. How's Elizabeth?"

"Same as ever. Still winding me up with fine artistry."

"Well, pass on my regards."

"I will. She's scheming all sorts of crap at home, you know. You should come visit. How's work?"

"Work is good," said Jack. "I'm coming along, and of course there's Dad's offer. Which I gather you know of?"

"Yeah, I mean, don't get me too deeply involved in that one. I think it's generally a good thing though. You've got potential. Would be good to know we're not doing all this for some immature schmuck to come along and fuck it up."

"Well, yes, there is that."

"There is, Jack. Which is why it means a lot to Alistair."

It was always Ray that Jack had spoken to about his troubles, and it was always Uncle Ray that got him out of them. Alistair would disdain the dirty work; Ray would roll up his sleeves, walk Jack to school, talk to the teachers who wanted to kick him out for smoking on school premises, talk some sense into the sixth-formers Jack owed money to for weed. It was Ray who Jack had cried in front of after a break-up; it was Ray who took him out to get him drunk and told him exactly why the girl had been so wrong for him. It was Ray who always seemed to make sense. So naturally, the conversation about Fran came to Uncle Ray.

"I've told him I'll give it some serious thought... Anyway, he doesn't need an answer right away."

"He's used to getting answers quickly though, and therein lies the issue."

Jack nodded and drank his beer. He hadn't eaten much for lunch, and he just knew that a few drinks would probably have a quick effect. His lager was already half-empty, his eagerness to drink it in stark contrast to his eagerness to talk about his father and his so-called plans for his empire.

There followed an easy back and forth as Ray bought up various topics. They spoke about the football, about Elizabeth wanting to build a water feature in the back garden, about Ray's new car, which was an amazingly beautiful Mercedes SL500 in silver and black. His eyes lit up as he spoke about the leather trim and the noise the engine made.

"Ray, I've met someone," said Jack abruptly.

"Well, I gathered the call for drinks might be down to that. Who is she?"

Jack laughed and moved his pint glass forward. "She's an older woman, Ray. Quite a bit older." He paused. "And unlike anyone I've met, really. Which is why I wanted your advice on… what you think I should do."

"Right. Okay." He sipped. "But, apart from the age thing, don't you think you're in a position now to make up your own mind on these things? "

Jack noticed the clock on the wall was showing the wrong time. "It's not that. It's… well, I'm feeling a lot of the feelings I had a long time ago. It's like a horrible impetuousness and, well, I… I don't know. You saw what I can get like."

Ray was silent for a short while. "Yes, I've seen what you can be like, but you were 18 and going through some shit; now you're a man with a good City career. They aren't the same two people."

Jack realised the clock had stopped. "It's not about that. It's about the same feelings. It's about not wanting to be vulnerable like that again. I don't want to be vulnerable."

"Who does? I was vulnerable when Liz bundled me a sack and married my ass."

"Ray." Jack's face stiffened up.

"Fine, okay, I admit that it took two of us. I'm just saying that I know you don't want to be vulnerable, but you're going to have to be that way if you're going in for the 'Big L'. Anyway, how many dates have you been on?"

"Three."

Ray looked back at Jack, surprised. "Three? And you're calling a conference already?"

"I've had this from Mickey."

"Mickey may look as thick as shit but he's a smart lad. And what did else he say?"

"That I needed to be careful. To play this one cooler than I would normally do."

"And I'd agree. I think that you should, to use a well-worn phrase, see *how it goes*."

"I am seeing how it goes."

"So, where do I come into it?"

"What do you think about the older woman part?"

"How old is she?"

"She's 38, or 39. I think 39."

Ray paused for longer than before. "That's a fair bit older than you. What happens if you want to have kids? What happens when you're forty yourself and in the prime of your career, busting out of your skin to get laid on your boat and she's claiming her bus pass?"

"Ray, this is not helping."

"Jack, this is the truth as it stands."

"I don't want to hear it."

"You might not want to hear the truth but it has an odd way of making itself quite relevant to your life."

Jack sighed. He was about to say something but instead took a big gulp of beer. The pub was full of men; he looked at a few of them. There was a haze in the air, the fug of the early evening. He couldn't believe that the things he thought about had any relevance to anybody there.

"I met her at Dad's club. She's called Francesca. She used to date the owner apparently."

From his usual calm demeanour, Ray visibly blanched and then struggled to look at Jack. More time passed than was normal as he tried to regain his composure and cover his reaction, However, Jack had noticed. "Ray? What's up?"

"Francesca, you say? You met her at Shore's?"

"Yes, why? Do you know her?"

"I… no, no. The name rings a bell, that's all." Jack looked at Ray and could see that he was lying. His face took on an aspect and Jack was like a son to him. The son that he'd never had. Jack realised that Ray knew something.

"Ray, who *is* Francesca? She's more than just Dave Shore's ex-girlfriend then?"

"No, no, that's how, how I knew the name. Your father and I have known Dave for a long time, and I guess I would have met her briefly at some point. Though he's always been fairly secretive about his women."

Jack looked at his drained expression. Ray was fidgeted with his empty pint of Guinness and Ray never fiddled with anything. He used to slap Jack around the back of this head when he fiddled with his drinks in pubs back when he was 17. "Are you bored?" he'd say. "Is this boring you?"

Ray was on his way to offering to buy a new round, but suddenly stopped short of saying anything. Jack decided to test the water. "Do you want to get another drink?"

"Um, I actually have to do some work with your father tonight. You know how much he'll hate me turning up all slow and full of Guinness. I'll have to pass, but I can get you one if you like."

Ray had turned up to his job interviews, to exams drunk. He'd met clients at two in the morning at Shore's and then woken up with some of the female ones in hotels across London. He was a consummate drinker. He wasn't going to turn down a pint with Jack unless there was a genuine reason behind it.

"Ray, what's the matter?"

"Nothing. Why don't you… tell me what this Francesca looks like?"

Jack noted Ray's turn of phrase. It was a little awkward

and more probing that he'd usually be.

"Sure. She's dark-haired and pale. Really pretty, with quite full cheeks and eyes, a little bit of green in them, but mostly blue. I'm sure there's a colour for it. She has a really good figure. She's about five-two, maybe five-three, quite curvy."

"That's… good, then."

"I thought you said it would be bad? That it would all head south in a few years and I'd be left sleeping with an old-aged-pensioner?"

"I didn't say that, Jack."

"Ray, what the hell's the matter? Do you know her? You've met her already, haven't you?" Jack paused. He looked at the wall while he waited for Ray to answer, but nothing came. "This is ridiculous, why would you hide information from me?" Jack was raising his voice and people at adjacent tables started looking round at them.

"Jack, I'm not hiding anything."

"You can't lie for shit, Ray. You couldn't lie to save your life. It's written all over your face. What is it? Did you date her? I guess you would have been attracted to her if she was at Shore's and you were there too. Is that it?"

Jack felt a keen wave of resentment and jealousy stir up. It was quite uncontrollable, like something primeval and primordial. He loved this man in front of him but suddenly the green-eyed monster was pulling back his ears and riding on his back, stamping into his mind images of Francesca and Ray.

"I would never have said more than two words to someone Dave Shore was going out with. He's the most jealous man we know."

"We know? So, what, did Dad know her too?"

"Jack, where are you getting to with all this?" Ray was flustered and their voices were now both raised. "I need you to calm down."

"You need to tell me what you're thinking Ray. No, not what you're thinking; what the fuck, tell me what you *know*."

"Stop this, Jack." Ray raised his own voice further and looked at Jack as forcefully as he'd ever done. There was menace in his growling imperative. "You need to stop right now with that tone."

"What tone?"

Ray was quieter. "Like you know what's best for you all the time. Because you know as well as I do that you haven't always been 24 and in a position to talk to me like you are now across a pub table."

"So you're pulling the older, wiser man act now? Without telling me what you know about Francesca?"

"Tell me how you met her."

Jack stopped, took a breath and answered Ray's question. "She was at Shore's; she was looking for someone. I've not asked her much more. We've spent most of our time, well, in *bed*." Jack broke out into a grin but it quickly subsided.

Ray looked at Jack. He studied his face. In many ways, it was like Alistair's, all about an aura of command and a naturally affinity for the sharp-cut suit. The eyes were different: Alistair's blank, whereas Jack's were alive, inquisitive.

Ray knew who Francesca was and what she'd been doing hanging around Shore's waiting to meet someone. And he was intensely worried about this turn of events.

"Jack, I have to go to meet your father; I'm going to be late as it is." He stood up.

"You said you were free for a drink, Ray?" Jack had lost a little of his angry edge and was now just a little confused. He recalled Fran's line and their lovemaking just the night before. He felt himself at sea with no rudder and he looked at Ray, who was now all set to leave, scooping his jacket up and grabbing his phone off the table. Jack's stomach was churning and his face was set.

"Jack, I will speak to you very soon about this. Just... look out for yourself, kiddo."

"Ray, you're acting really strangely."

"Yes, I know, I'm... under some stress. I – " Ray faltered. He held out his hand and Jack took it. "I am just feeling a little under pressure from Alistair."

Ray's lies were written all over his face. The lies hurt the most, the misinformation, the wilful distortion of the truth. Jack felt his resistance ebb away.

"I'll see you then."

"Yes, very soon."

Ray headed out of the pub, at pace. Jack got his phone out of his pocket and sent a text to Fran asking her if he could come round. He finished his beer and the reply buzzed in his pocket just as walked through the door and into the rapidly cooling night. Blur's 'Charmless Man' kicked in just as he left.

'Yes, come round, am waiting for you x' flashed up on his display.

He headed to the Tube station and the complexities of his situation began to increase.

Ray got a cab and told the driver to head to Alistair's address, picking up the phone to call ahead.

"Hi Al. It's Ray."

"Yes, I know, your name comes up on the phone like everyone else's."

"Cute. I need to talk to you about Jack."

"Jack? What's he done?"

"Something that affects us all, I think. Just get out of whatever you have to do and I'll be at yours very soon. This needs to be done face-to-face."

"Face-to-face? Sure. I'll see you in a little while."

He clicked off, and Ray put the phone into his jacket pocket, brushing his hair with his fingers. The cab driver was silent for once and Ray leaned into the seat, sighing, watching the lights go by in the gathering gloom. Jack had stepped into a world not of his making.

PART II

1

Ray's black cab pulled up at Alistair's house. He handed the driver a crisp note through the window and waved away the change with a half-raised hand. He turned to walk through the gate and up the long path of the impressive Wilson residence. Ray's own house was more modest, a Georgian townhouse. This on the other hand was a work that mirrored what Alistair Wilson thought of himself, that people should walk a while before they could get to him and the distance was a chance for him to get their measure.

Ray pulled his coat around himself a little tighter and hit the buzzer. A light came on at the top of the console and he imagined a mini-CCTV system spring to life. A camera focussing on his face, heavy set and square; picking out the crispness of his new white shirt. The lock opened and Ray stepped in, pushing the heavy wooden door open and then letting it shut behind him with a metallic clunk. Alistair appeared, still dressed as if for the office, with a tumbler of what looked like whisky and ice. He had a pair of pinstripe trousers and a white shirt with his sleeves rolled up. Pleats fitted it round his toned frame and the dark blue tie was slightly loosened in a concession to the hour.

"Shall we take it to the kitchen and I'll get you a drink?" asked Alistair.

"Sure," said Ray, and he followed as they crossed the hall, turned right into a small corridor and took the first left into a spacious, modern kitchen. Alistair hit a switch and halogen bulbs came on, dim at first and then blindingly bright when looked at directly. Alistair moved to the cupboard and got out a tumbler, taking it over to the fridge and filling it with ice. There was a bottle of single malt on the worktop and he poured a fairly generous measure into it. Alistair bought it over to Ray, who'd sat up at the breakfast bar, his elbows now on the granite worktop and the cold of the stone starting to get a little uncomfortable quite quickly.

"So, what is this big problem that we have?" said Alistair.

Ray paused, weighing his words carefully. After some consideration, he decided to just come out with it.

"Francesca Darlington is sleeping with your son, Alistair."

Alistair looked Ray directly in the eyes, but the shock on his face was unmistakable. He struggled to say anything and finally took the defensive.

"This is a joke, right, Ray? A joke – a good one, but you can tell me exactly why you made it after I've finished smacking your face."

"Al, it's not a joke." Ray stiffened and looked right back at Alistair. There was a nervous silence that lasted at least thirty seconds. Ray took a huge gulp of whisky.

"So, are you going to tell me how this... happened?" Alistair finished the whisky in his glass, took Ray's almost empty tumbler and refilled them across the kitchen. As he walked back, Ray started to explain.

"I met up with him for a drink. And he mentioned this new girl that he met at Shore's. He wanted some relationship advice because she was an older woman. And I asked for details and it's pretty likely to be Francesca."

"You're not entirely sure then?"

"I haven't got photographic proof, but all the signals ring true and it appears she was back in town looking for us. At Shore's. Instead she met Jack. That night you met him there to talk some more about the offer." Ray paused. "And she might have known, or might not have known, but, being as they're four dates in, are they likely to know each other's surnames?"

"That night he took liberties with my tab. I thought it was too much for him to have drunk alone. The little shit."

"He was just picking up a girl he liked and, as I said, I don't even know if she knows."

"Knows what?"

"That Jack is your son."

"Oh come off it. You think she wouldn't twig, meeting a 'Jack Wilson' who looks a bit like the older Alistair Wilson, at the same club where we'd have secret drinks in the back room when we were all up in London?"

"The thought has crossed my mind."

"Well, that's brilliant Ray. Good to know your faculties are still firing on all cylinders."

"Why are you shooting the messenger, Al? You just always get on this fucking high horse. Did I *engineer* this?"

Alistair looked down at the granite worktop blankly. He put his hands down on it and exhaled, slowly.

Ray spoke again. "I don't think she'd be that scheming, Alistair."

"You don't? Time changes people."

"She was a precocious girl that we took to some dark places. We left her, Alistair, and she never came back; she just walked away. With a baby, Alistair. *Your* baby."

"Keep your voice down, Ray," said Alistair, with no small

hint of menace.

"I'm hardly likely to spill the beans now after, all these years."

"Why would she come back then, when she had been so resolved to go away?"

"I don't know."

"It's been twenty years!"

"Twenty-three actually. I remember when she walked off. I spent that year thinking we'd be hit by a paternity suit." Ray looked down at his own hands. "She never spilled. And we never offered to help. Not one bit."

"Is guilt the right emotion after nearly a quarter century?"

"I think something about it is appropriate," said Ray.

"So I should be penitent even now?"

"I'm not asking you to shoulder the entire burden."

"My kid, though, right? You'll not let that one drop."

"Everyone has let it drop, Alistair. It's you that keeps this alive."

"You, me and her that keep it alive more like. My illegitimate child who keeps it alive, more to the point." Alistair paused for a long time. "Why is she back, then?"

"Maybe because people want answers."

"After this amount of time?"

"People want to know why."

"Take your philosophy and fuck off, Ray. I really don't want to speak to you about this anymore today."

Ray looked up, angrily. "You selfish prick, Alistair. This is your son. Going with a woman who gave birth to his *half-sibling*. And here you are, as usual, wrapped up in your own problems. Step up to the plate, you coward. For your son."

"You don't really have the right to talk to me about sons."

Ray felt the fury begin to build. "I have as much right as you because he thinks of me as more of a father than you've ever been. With your moods, your short shrift and your fucking ridiculous ideas of *honour*. After all that you've done. Honour. Don't make me laugh at you, Alistair. I won't be able to stop."

They both got off their stools. "Where is this heading, Ray? To you getting a swift right hook?"

"If you end up fighting me here, Alistair, you'll be waking up in a hospital, and I'm not joking. And you don't want to end up with a broken face when Jack needs you."

"And you love him so much, right? More than I did?"

"I've just never known what your kind of love was exactly. I'm sure it's there somewhere. Gnarled and twisted."

"You're a piece of work, Ray. With your failed dreams and broken marriage."

Ray looked at him intently, then broke the stare, eyes heading downwards to the worktop again. They sat down slowly and lapsed into silence. The noises of the kitchen took over, the ticking of a clock and the hum of electrical appliances.

Finally, Alistair spoke. "What are we going to do?"

"We… should probably start off by speaking to Fran. If we can get out of this with Jack not knowing who he's sleeping with, that's a fair bit of damage limitation."

"Agreed." Alistair got up off the stool and looked towards the door, as if that would create the world of action right there.

"And so we need to find out where she's staying and go and see her as soon as we can."

"Will you call the relevant people?" asked Alistair.

"I'll do it tonight, yes."

"Good."

"Perhaps we should have lunch tomorrow and work out where we'll take this? I don't feel comfortable talking about it here." Instinctively, Ray felt a small surge of nostalgia for the days when the two of them had been action figures with boundless energy, barking orders at each other and bouncing plans and schemes back and forth.

"Okay. Meet me at Reviens at 1pm?"

"I'll see myself out."

"Did you come here in a cab?"

"I'll get one from the station."

"Let me drive you down."

"It's a five minute walk, Alistair."

"I bought some new driving gloves." He flashed a rare smile, which soon faded. "I appreciate you telling me this so quickly."

"I think it concerns both of us, really."

"Yes, but it's a mess and it's going to get quickly out of hand if we don't deal with it as soon as we can. If – *people* find out. It could be – bad for me. For us both. I doubt Elizabeth would – like it any more than Rachel would." He moved slowly through the sentence, which was unlike him.

"Let's go to the station," said Ray, leading the way to the garage.

2

It was the next day. A clock somewhere nudged towards 1pm. Alistair walked briskly into a restaurant that looked as if had been hewn out of wood and granite, thick-set and ponderous. Reviens wasn't known to do things by halves. Ray was sat in a corner booth, a beer in front of him in a glass tankard taken from a freezer and still partially-frosted. He looked up and met Alistair's gaze, eyes then dipping back to a menu that both were familiar with.

Alistair pulled back a chair and sat down, gruffly saying "hello" and letting his hand drift to his tie, a charcoal grey with thin diagonal black stripes, shifting it a few millimetres.

"The tie was fine where it was," said Ray.

"I think we can dispense with the jocular and quotidian, Baxbury. This is about some pressing business."

Ray let the heavy and dour remark hang in the air for a while before he replied. "I remember – you know, it wasn't so long ago – I remember you being a wonderful, funny man."

"I remember when you remembered correctly. Don't get me confused with any of your new-found mid-life crisis running buddies."

"Time was, I didn't need them."

"Time was, is and will be," said Alistair.

"Oh, go fuck yourself, Wilson."

The chair that Alistair sat on made a creaking sound as he shifted his weight back and put his hands behind his head. Just a few seconds later, a waiter appeared and asked if they were ready to order. Alistair went for the medium steak and then, after glancing at Ray's now nearly empty pint glass, ordered two glasses of red wine. Ray ordered a well-done steak.

"Certainly," the waiter said, turning and walking off with a practiced gait that blended archness with efficiency.

"Did you sleep all right last night?" asked Ray, one hand reaching for his beer and helping the last part of it down.

"No," answered Alistair, his head tilting to the right as if buffeted by some imperceptible wind.

"Me neither. Although part of my concern wasn't just about this, um, situation."

"What was it about then? The global plight of panda bears?"

"It was about you, Al. About the last few years in general. About what happened to the man that used to be, unequivocally, my best friend."

"You're asking these questions now?"

"I'm asking now because it's dawned on me that I finally want – and deserve – some answers. Maybe this situation is the tipping point."

"We both grew up, Ray. We're not doing drugs at beach parties anymore. Surely the lines on your face have told you that much?" Alistair paused. "And we're not start-up businessmen with no capital. Did you not get the memo?"

"Why trivialise this – when it's deeper than that?"

"Stop doing this."

"Doing what? Doing *what?* I'm tired of your gnomic bullshit, Alistair. You think you're a curt, middle-aged stud, when really you're a lonely, short-tempered old fuck."

Ray's voice had risen with his increasing annoyance.

"Keep your voice down, Raymond."

"You think they don't know, too? We've been coming here years. They've seen it too."

"Who is 'they'? The bricks? The tables?"

Ray paused and took a breath. It was a maze of dead-ends. "Let's talk about Fran."

"Yes. Let's do that."

"What do you think we should do?"

Alistair paused as the waiter came over, all senses tilting to the gossip, the conspiratorial. He placed two glasses of wine on the table. "Thank you," said Ray, as the waiter left. Both took time to take a sip and break off a little of the bread that had also arrived. Ray buttered his slowly as Alistair spoke.

"Well, we should probably make a decision fairly quickly, because we don't know if this woman that you said is Fran is planning to do anything crazy."

"Al, I've thought about it, checked, and the woman is definitely Fran. I'll do a visual when I see her, but I would put money on it. All the signs point to it."

"So you think that you should be the one to make contact?"

"I think that you doing it would be a very bad idea."

"And you want to do it in person?"

"I think the surprise element will be important."

A pause. Other diners were talking about their days, a gentle rolling noise in the background. The oiled cogs of the everyday. The corner table was made into a kind of booth by the walls and it was out of earshot. Ray liked this place, its food and the fact that they knew the owners. They managed to get whichever table suited their purpose, from that one at the back to the front ones near the busy main road. Middle-class mothers gripping lattes pushed their children down the pavements in oversized, armoured buggies. He tried to catch their eyes, these days failing more often than not. What had happened to him?

"And from the way you're talking –"

"Yes, I have an address," interrupted Ray, head still in the previous thought. "I got my friend to run some searches on various databases. She's on a short stay leave in a North-East London flat. She obviously had to fill out some form or other and all this shit seems to end up in the same places. She didn't use any kind of false name."

"Francesca Darlington," said Alistair, letting the syllables linger.

"The very same."

"She's not trying to hide, then?"

"Why would anyone be looking for her?"

"Why wouldn't they, after she makes an uninvited appearance at Shore's?"

"You make it sound like she broke the law? She must have wanted to find *you*, Al. And now, conversely, *you* have to find *her*."

"I have contact details all over the place, why turn up at Shore's on the off-chance I might be there?"

"I think she'd have wanted to run into you, rather than make a fucking business appointment to discuss twenty years of silence?"

"Which changes the motive?"

"You're thinking about some confused notion of backdated alimony?"

"Maintenance, yes. That's what crossed my mind. She's run into money troubles, big ones, and comes to me when pride runs out in the face of need."

"I think," said Ray, leaning in, "that you might not be thinking as clearly as you should be."

"Why?"

"If she wanted maintenance, or even hush money, why would she currently be all doe-eyed with your *son*? I think that is the key and rather sick part of events that you have failed to grasp."

"I just – haven't – really got to that bit yet." Alistair paused again and there some was a degree of confusion that broke through the usually composed expression.

"Al. Look at me," said Ray. Alistair looked up. "This is a *very* strange situation. I don't expect you to be quite on top of it yet, and I know as well that you're not going to admit any weakness." He paused and Alistair broke his gaze, looking away almost too quickly, his eyes squinting. "So, I'm going to go and see Fran and find out exactly what is happening, before we do anything else."

"That seems like a good idea."

"And the gist of what I'll say is that Jack can*not* learn about who she is, and that she needs to leave him, and us, well alone."

"Yes."

"Also, that she needs to talk to you. It's been too long, Alistair."

Alistair looked back up at Ray, and then around as the waiter arrived with the two steaks, fat chips lining the plates.

"Your food, gentlemen," said the waiter, putting the medium one in front of Alistair and the well-done one on Ray's side of the table. He hung around just long enough for them to raise any possible issues and then headed off back to the kitchen.

Ray exhaled. "I'm waiting for you to get angry, Alistair."

"I am angry already. It's just that I'm so angry, it hasn't even had a chance to percolate."

"Do you want to maybe give me a précis?"

"I'd rather eat some of this steak first."

Ray smiled and they managed to take a few bites, but neither was really that hungry. The spectre of a season that occurred over twenty years ago was back with them.

Francesca Darlington was a young girl who'd been brought to a beach party at the house that Ray and Alistair had hired on the coast as a weekend get-away. She'd tagged along with a young teenage boy, ostensibly as his date. He'd puked after a few cans of beer and before 8pm lay glazed next to an upturned deck chair. She was eager, impossibly attractive, and had managed, even then, to pace herself.

She'd walked right up to Alistair, who was leaning into Ray and telling him a story about a work colleague, standing there until both were forced to look at her. She had dark-brown hair and eyes that were blue and grey, and impossible to ignore. She was wearing a wrap, over a beach bikini that she just about managed to fill.

"I guess you're the people who are renting the house, then?" she'd said, speaking crisply and straight at Alistair. In his mid-twenties, a wife in tow, her trying for a child, in that instant he felt the binds of the office and of a frosted glass home life drift away.

"Yes. I'm Alistair Wilson and this is my friend, John Raymond Baxbury."

"Call me Ray," he said, extending his hand. The single one of the two, Ray jumped up and took another look at her in a new light. She was impossibly young, and his heart sank a little. Life was complicated. People milled around on the patch of beach that the house extended onto, the rear garden turning into golden sand and sea. It was a hot day that had turned into a warm and mellow evening.

"How's your young friend?" asked Ray.

"He's comatose," she said, smiling. Alistair felt his heart

skip at her precociousness.

"I'll fix you a proper drink," said Ray, heading over to the wet bar they'd set up on the beach and beckoning her on. "And introduce you to some people younger than us."

As she walked away, she pierced Alistair with a gaze that he could still remember twenty-five years on, in a warm and comfortable restaurant eating an expensive steak. The years were collapsing around his carefully constructed fences and walls. There was no compartmentalisation.

As Fran walked off two decades ago, Ray faded in, a fork in the air, making a point about that night.

"Al? You with me?"

"Yes. Go on."

Ray very faintly smiled, and then said, "I'm going to go round at about seven tonight and see if she's in, okay?"

"Sooner is better, yes."

"Do you have any idea what Jack might be up to?"

"Not really."

"We need to find out if he is seeing her tonight. I can't risk turning up and he's there. You need to invite him out for a drink. An important drink. Tell him that you've something of vital importance to say – make something up and just act drunk when he turns up, say you've forgotten. Whatever. If he's not seeing her, chances are she'll be in." Ray paused, brain racing. "As a back up, I need you to wait until Jack goes to the toilet and get Fran's number from his phone. It might be quite hard and, if he's carrying his phone with him, you'll just have to use your imagination."

"That sounds pretty difficult."

"Alistair – this is a difficult situation."

"I'm already worried about the possibility of Rachel finding out."

Rachel. His wife had been at home that weekend, visiting friends, doing the rounds as a married, moneyed suburban London lady of leisure. Alistair's wages allowed her to leave her job, paid for the house and paid for pretty much everything. He'd gotten her a small sports car that she drove around. She was supposed to be seeing her friend Jennifer, having lunch in town and then looking at household appliances with her at some department store or other.

Years ago, he'd tell her he was going down to the House on the Coast with Ray, and he'd always come back a little worn from hedonism, smelling of the sea and trailing sand in with his weekend bags. Ray had been his friend since university, his best man. A great silent witness to any infidelities.

The guilt hit him hardest at first, but he got over it by pretending it didn't matter, that everyone was doing it, and, to be honest, pretty much every man he knew in the office was. There was money moving around and girls were impressed by money, by power, by those things in abundance when attached to youth and vigour. He thought he was wise to all of that. Most of the time, he just got too fucked to bother with it anyway. He loved Rachel, loved her dearly, loved the mind-blowing sex with this beautiful woman who would rip his favourite shirts to piss him off and go wild on the anger and the lust. He could never understand why he felt something was missing when in fact nothing was. With his slim figure and good-looks, his expensive suits and sharp brain, his capacity for drink and drugs and no sleep, why was anything missing? Perhaps he wanted something to be missing so had a reason to go on seeking? He would never be happy with his lot because he'd shoot holes in the hull himself. Ray wasn't like Alistair. With his stocky build and shock of hair, he was a tank of a man. He was also more steady and relaxed than Alistair could ever be. He'd sit and play board games with the slow tenacity of a heavyweight, smiling a slow smile as the Jack and Coke worked its way through his system.

When Fran turned up at the party that night he made moves to take her away from Alistair, sensing the tension, the spark. He took her to the wet bar on wheels and made her a gin and tonic, trying to make small talk and to redirect her to the youths that remained standing. Her original companion was still slumped in the corner and had a dumb smile spread across his face.

"So, you're called Francesca, then?"

"Yes, Francesca Darlington. Usually Fran."

"And Fran, how *old* are you exactly?" He looked at her keenly, eyes meeting eyes.

"Seventeen," she said, without missing a beat.

Ray let the lie run. "That's nice. How's the G and T?"

"It's – fine. A little strong, maybe."

"I can put some more tonic in, if you like."

"Just another ice cube should do it," she said, coquettishly. She held out her drink with an exaggerated motion, arm ending up bent back a little on itself and the drink becoming the focus and nexus of some hidden debate. To do, or not to do, to believe or not to believe?

"What brings you here, Fran?" asked Ray, putting an extra ice cube in the drink and swishing it round.

"I came with Gareth over there, but he's… indulged himself a little too much."

"You've got a nice command of vocabulary, Fran."

"Well, maybe I was sent to a good school?"

"Maybe schools don't often teach party chat and insouciant gestures?"

"I don't follow, John."

"It's Ray. John Raymond Baxbury. Everyone calls me Ray."

"John Raymond Baxbury, huh? That's some name." Her full stops were heavy and full. He struggled to give the conversation some inertia.

"I didn't really have much of a say in it, Francesca."

"Is this where you let me return to Alistair?" Her eyes were burning into him. He felt himself stir. It was a game that he was losing despite his own inner sense of security, despite his age advantage and experience. He couldn't fully understand the plays that were unfolding. The evening breeze blew across his face, whipping some sand into his right eye.

"Argh, bloody – sand," he said, wiping frantically at the eye to no avail. He squinted at Fran with his other eye. She was unmoved and watching him carefully. "I'm going to have to go inside and wash this out, so go ahead and talk to Al if you wish."

"I will."

"Good," he said, moving off in the direction of the house, a little unsteadily and holding the right side of his face with his right hand.

He often tried not to remember the way things turned out after that. Do things turn on a pin-head, a grain of sand, the gust of a breeze? Maybe the tectonic plates of the events that conspire are much more determined that we allow ourselves to admit.

He got back to the party and a girl took his arm and made him slow-dance to something playing over the grey and silver boom box that was already dug a few inches into the sand.

He kept stealing glances to Alistair, who was regaling Fran with story after story. Her laugh tinkled around in broken echoes with the thick sea air carrying it over the crackle of a fire and the laughing of the assembled. He gave up on the dance when the girl started to nibble his ear; he let go of her. She felt his face with her left hand and looked at him, half there and half on some other planet from the amount of weed she'd smoked already. Her keening eyes weren't altogether unattractive, but he was distracted, and a little disturbed.

Fran was tucked in Alistair's neck and Ray felt the jealousy rise up and throw a sheet over his head, pulling the drawstrings tight. He gasped, involuntarily, and the girl, Maisy, noticed something was wrong. It seemed to bring her out of her blissed-out state.

"Are you okay, Ray?"

"Yes, I'm fine. Do – you – want another drink?"

She laughed and said yes. He looked inwards and found shards of glass.

"I'll get one." He got up and made his way to the bar. He wasn't a jealous man. He loved Alistair. But Fran was somehow disturbing the fabric. He hated having his nature altered by someone else. He looked for some accountancy in all of it. The sums, the columns, the rigorous arithmetic of reason. He broke rank for just a second. What was the girl doing there? They'd passed partners between them before and always came through any situation with a clear demarcation of who was whose. Ever since the days at university in sticky-floored bars, the intuition had never failed them. But something was wrong.

He looked back at himself, about to turn and head over to Alistair, but caught it in the moment. He paced to the bar and made two strong whisky and cokes. He handed one to Maisy when he got back.

"Shall we go inside? It's getting a little cold," he said, to a girl who was wearing nothing more than a bikini despite the sea breeze whipping in and the sun having set a while ago.

Back in Reviens, Alistair motioned to the waiter for two more glasses of wine.

"I probably should have gotten a bottle."

"Well, that's my general rule."

"I meant for both of us, though."

"Ah."

They both smiled. There was still something alive in Alistair, despite the cold front that had lasted for years. His own son had drifted away, never getting what he needed, or even getting close to the real Alistair. Ray thought it was a shame that Jack thought of him as more of a father than Alistair. Then, however, there were plenty of those cases across the country, across the world. Fathers letting down sons, interested in other things, the keen fascination of hobbies, addictions, vices and leisure. Breaking away from the pure arithmetic.

They'd woken up that day, strewn across the living room, Ray noting with dread Fran being spooned by a dishevelled Alistair on the huge futon in the corner. Maisy was on his shoulder, her blond hair tangled up and her breathing shallow. Ray hadn't slept with her.

Later, in the kitchen, when the guests had returned to their lives: "Do you know how young she is, Alistair?"

"What?" he'd said, still a little drunk, smiling.

"She's probably fifteen, Alistair. If that."

"She said she was seventeen."

"She's very mature for her age, I'll give her that. Did you sleep with her?"

Alistair paused. "Yes, I did."

"And you used protection."

"Yes, I did, Ray. Now can I make a coffee?"

He let him make a coffee. Fran came back, again and

again; Ray would sit through the evenings, unable to place his emotions. Eventually, she was pregnant with Alistair's child.

3

It was around six-thirty and Ray was driving his car to the address he'd been given for Fran. He'd been in touch with Alistair by text; Jack had taken the bait and was meeting him at a pub near High Holborn for some 'important' chat over drinks. The plan was that Alistair would act in a state of incoherence when he got there, and sober up over the course of the evening, hopefully keeping Jack there long enough. Fran would then hopefully be in the flat and, even if she was out, she would at least be nowhere near Jack.

Ray would later send a text to Alistair to tell him if they needed to get hold of Fran's mobile number from Jack's phone. If he saw her, Ray was to read the riot act: coming back was a step firmly in the wrong direction, and sleeping with Jack was some sort of sick high-stakes game played in entirely the wrong spirit.

The flat was on the first floor. He'd bought a box of tricks to help get past the door lock but now he was going to have to get past an electronic lock too. He parked the car up near the flat, around the corner, and took a breath. Shutting the car door, he bleeped his central locking on and tried to open up his body language. Sure enough, someone popped out of the flat as he headed in, having hung about for a few minutes smoking a cigarette.

He smiled and they didn't ask any questions – this was a city, after all. He let the door shut and took a short jog up the stairs to the right door. He decided that the first thing to do would be to knock, but suddenly he was stopped by a sense of how random this whole thing was. What would he actually say and what would he do?

He knocked after pulling his collars up and flatting out his body language once again. There was a noise from the other side of the door and he noticed someone check the spy hole. Then there was a voice, warm and clear, slightly muffled by the door and the insulation around it.

"Who is it?" The tone was laced with prior recognition.

"It's – Ray, Fran. Raymond Baxbury."

There was a pause of some seconds. The seconds turned into half a minute, and Ray found himself having to speak again.

"Francesca. I found you through some detective work and, well, I'm here to talk to you."

"Right, I believe that, *Ray*." Her voice. He recognised it. But it was deeper, naturally. And it hadn't retained that sense of sureity.

"Well, believe what you like, but I would like to talk to you."

"Okay, we can talk like this."

"Not really. It's of a fairly personal nature."

"A personal nature with regards to me, or to you?"

"With regards to us all."

"I see. So, I suppose you know about Jack and me, then?"

Ray paused, and considered what he should say. "And that leads me to believe that you know that Jack is Alistair's *son*, Fran. Does that not mean we should talk, as in fairly promptly?" He was starting to lose his cool against a locked door, which wasn't a good sign. He'd not been in many of these situations. He'd had to knock on a few doors after hours in the early days of his business career, usually as a favour for a favour. But this was a whole new thing to him. His mind kept flitting back to a gin and tonic at a wet bar, an overstated gesture, to waking up in a room with the sun filtering through the windows. Him waking up next to a blonde, a brunette, waking up to a pair of breasts or the flat chest of some thin girl that had grown tired of surfers.

He remembered the panic strewn acknowledgments of Fran's pregnancy. Her bullish pride and the way she slowly closed off to them both. The sought confessions of tacit silence. Her spitting out words drenched in violence at a panic-stricken Alistair. The fact she'd slept with him too; out of boredom and spite. The fact that Alistair only knew through half-gestures and shrugs of complacent denial. The silence had stretched through too many years.

"Let me in Fran, please. I need to talk to you."

"Okay," she said, and she turned the lock. She pulled the door back and he saw a woman grown up out of the girl he'd known. The same bone structure and clear complexion, the same deep and engaging eyes. Lines that had settled around her face and it held the knowingness of age and experience. He didn't know what to do and so stood there, immobile in a heavy leather jacket, smelling of fresh cigarette smoke and gum.

"Fran."

"Ray."

"Should I? – I'll, um."

"Come in. Sit down." She was curt, looking at him watchfully and with a sense of careful knowing.

"Okay." He went on through and took in his surroundings. The flat was fairly small and oddly tidy in parts. This was balanced by magazines and papers forming mini-stacks on the floor. Some of her clothes were draped on the backs of chairs, on her sofa. Heartbreakingly, he spotted one of Jack's shirts. There was a smell of fresh laundry. A window that was open meant a breeze blew through until she shut the front door. He didn't move or sit down, but turned to face her.

"It's been a long, long time, Francesca."

"Yes, it has. I guess I could stretch to a coffee while you think about what it is you want to say." She walked off towards the kitchen. His eyes naturally fell onto her figure, as if it was the only thing to do. It was fuller, obviously, but retained its dimensions. The elegant curves of her body, the pinched waist; her hair was as dark as it had been all those years ago. The kitchen, in contrast to the living room, was very orderly, devices tucked away into their respective places. She switched on a non-descript coffee machine and took some cups out of the cupboard. She opened the fridge to get the coffee and hammered out the used up grinds. There were some stools placed near what could be called a break-fast bar, so he moved towards her, pulled one out and sat down.

"I came here to talk to you about Jack, Francesca."

"That's what I gathered from you at the door. What about it?" She kept herself busy at the coffee machine, not turning to look at him.

"About you and him."

"Go on."

"You're not going make this easy, are you?" He paused, exhaled. "I came here to talk to you about you having a relationship with the son of a man that you had a child with over twenty years ago. A child you had when you were hopelessly underage. And, despite whatever acrimony there was at the end, a child that is Jack's *half-sibling*, Fran!"

She fiddled with some settings, then turned to him. "Jack's

no blood relation of mine, before you start with that tack. And the child was a boy."

Ray paused to take in the news. Alistair had another son. "There is no tack, Fran."

"Right." She turned back and carried on.

"Yes, right. I'm right in that this is all very, very wrong."

"Ah, still with the *bon mots*, I see. Sugar?"

"Yes, one sugar, please."

She stirred a sugar into his espresso, turned and placed the cup near where he sat.

"No saucers, I'm afraid. And no biscotti, either."

He wanted to smile back at her, match the smile she'd given him. It was, however, a forced one. He tried to remain on track. "Fran, could we maybe talk about how this all started? Why you came back, for example? And where you met Jack? And how you managed to get together with the half-brother of your... son?"

"You don't sound at all as if you practised that little cascade of questions."

"Yes, well, maybe I had to, Fran. Maybe that was the only way I'd remember to stick to the script with someone who doesn't want to explain herself."

"Why should I have to explain any of my actions to you, or to *Alistair*? You are two people I washed my hands of years ago."

"Then what were you doing at Shore's, Fran?" She stopped whatever it was she was about to say and looked at him. He carried on. "Shore's, where you helped Jack run up a lovely tab but couldn't possibly have been there to meet him. There are two people you might have wanted to see. Shorey himself, but he's most often out of town and in any case I doubt it was him." He drank a little coffee. It was good, and strong. "Or Alistair Wilson, who's been going there for years and years?"

"I wasn't looking for him."

"Then it was a trip down memory lane? After two-and-a-half decades?"

"It was nothing. I wanted a drink."

"In an exclusive member's bar that you had to sign into? I checked. You somehow managed *not* to sign in."

"I snuck in."

"Past the door?"

"It's not so hard with a good bra, okay? I told them I was there to meet Alistair Wilson."

"So now we get to it."

"They didn't mark that into their precious little log book?"

"They did."

"So why all of these questions? When you know all of this already?"

"Fran – I just want to know why you came back, for starters. After all this time, when you could have come back whenever, when you could have made Alistair pay child support for years, could have called a local paper, could have even called *him*? Why?" He raised his hands to add to the question, holding them there until they were too obvious, too forced, too much of a theatrical device. So he raked them back through his hair and exhaled, then took his coffee up again.

She was silent for a long time. He heard the coffee machine cool down and the drip of a tap that hadn't been tightened. A siren went past on the road outside. Still, she said nothing. He guessed that she was weighing up a further pretence versus the one thing she had always traded in. Brutal, truthful punches – even back then, an insouciant teen with a passion for invective.

"I came back because he has to acknowledge Sean."

Ray, in turn, took a long time to respond. "Sean."

"He is the same age as Jack."

"Then does that not –"

"You know Jack, right?" She was leaning forward. She wanted to get her point across.

"Better than Alistair does. He's like a son to me."

"Then you know that it's like meeting Alistair, but with all the bad bits taken away?"

"The thought has crossed my mind, but –"

"He was there. He was there, this man, this person, just like, it was." She didn't say anything for a long time and let whatever it was she wanted to say hang in the air. "Just like *he* was."

She bit her lip and he knew she was suddenly on the verge of tears. He didn't do anything for a long while, while she sat there, composing herself, and then letting herself continue. She seemed very on edge. He knew if he made a single move to comfort her, she'd slap him, or worse. Finally, he said something. "But he's not, and this isn't, and it can't be, Fran."

"Jack is what he could have been. I didn't mean to meet him there. I didn't know who he was. He just looked similar. He was at a table. I saw him, he just –"

She tailed off. The incredulity of it all hit Ray and he veered from his intended route.

"Fran, he doesn't just look *similar*. He's the spitting image of Al, and you must have known. He's a great kid, Fran, even after twenty years of Alistair slowly freezing up into a fucking statue."

Ray got up, off the stool, and put the coffee cup in the sink. He came back to his chair and put his hands through his hair again. "You're going to absolutely fuck him up, and I mean that. I've not seen him like this, about anyone. He's spoken to *me*, about *you*. About *you*, Fran! Our beach house secret from back before he was born. Now, how fucking weird is that? And how shitty is it going to be if it all comes out? How sick will he feel?"

"What are you talking about?"

"He's sleeping with the *mother of his half-brother*, Fran. He is sleeping with his father's *ex-concubine*." He laid a stress on the last word. He had said it because he needed to raise the pitch, make the situation clear. There had to be a resolution because this couldn't become some tea party with everyone talking to each other, as if this were a normal day during a normal course of events.

She locked eyes with him, narrowing them. Finally, it clicked. "Fuck you, Ray! Fuck *you* and the horse you rode in on, you're still the *same*, you, you, *cunt*! You were the insidious whispering *cunt* at his side, Ray. You sent him back to his wife and your boring jobs. Fuck *you*! Get out of my flat!"

"You were fifteen, Francesca!" he shouted back. He held her gaze. "*Fif-teen*! You should have had an abortion and lived the rest of your life, gone to university, gotten a career. You –"

Fran stood up from her stool, pushed her weight into her movement and slapped him as hard as she could across the face. He pitched to the side. She left finger marks deep across his left cheek, and he stood there, stunned. He put up a hand to his cheek, and felt blood slowly drip down it.

"You've cut me, Fran."

"Good! I hope you bleed to death right here."

"Fran, what's… what's happened to you? To bring you here? To bring this back to our table?"

"The choices I made were mine to make, okay? I wanted to have Sean. I wanted my baby. And I've never regretted it. I don't regret not becoming some frustrated career woman banging her head on a glass ceiling. And, why am I here?" She stopped to take a breath and look at what she'd done to

Ray's face. He had livid finger marks across his left cheek. "I wanted Sean to meet his father; that's all, okay? That's what I came back for. I think he has a right. I didn't mean to meet Jack and I – I didn't mean for him to meet me. This is a complication I hadn't factored in."

Ray held his hand to his face and leaned into it. He closed his eyes and winced. The blood was coming out more evenly now and some had dripped down his face onto his white shirt collar.

"Factored in, a nice phrase." He could feel a wave of pain from his face. "Do you have a box of tissues, or something? A plaster?"

"I'm sorry."

"About the missing box of tissues? Or my cut up face?"

"Your face. I didn't mean to cut you."

"No, of course not." It was stinging quite badly. He sat back down on the stool and put his face in his hands. When he looked up, Fran had disappeared into the bathroom. She came back with some iodine and a set of bandages and plasters. For a moment they considered the scene. Would he be the wincing hero, would Fran play the love interest dabbing a wound, his reaction to the stinging antiseptic out of all proportion? She thrust the pack out to him and pointed out the bathroom.

"Go and clean yourself up, Ray. You're making a mess of your shirt."

He walked to the bathroom, put the iodine and plasters down on the windowsill behind the basin. The sun was low in the sky, right behind the flat, shining in. He ran the tap, getting a cool, even flow and then splashed water onto his face. The cut stung as the water came into contact with it and he tried to run his finger down it to gauge its size and depth. His hands came away red. In the mirror, he saw the damage, then saw his own face, the tired face of a man in his late-forties. There was the day-old stubble, the patches under his eyes. He grabbed a towel from the rack and dried his hands.

The cut would scab up soon enough. He grabbed some of the toilet roll, folded it up, and put it onto the cut to soak up the blood. The bathroom was painted a neutral blue, with mostly white fittings. A female razor was suction-cupped to the tiles around the bath to his left. It hurt to look at it for too long, picturing it running down her thighs. The frosted window made the light hazy. Where should he go now? Where would the conversation turn? He'd said his piece and told her what he wanted her to do, and somehow it had turned into this. Ray decided to walk out after asking her to do the right thing, to leave Jack alone and to not tell him any of the back-story. He'd ask her to speak to Alistair. He'd walk away because his own marriage was faltering, his own life was somehow stuttering like the motorbike in his garage he couldn't fix, its imposing mass like some physical manifestation of his mid-life crisis. While Alistair had iced up, slowly getting more studied and more arch, Ray had let his familiar smile and easy manner be replaced by something he sometimes couldn't recognise. Who was he?

He walked back into the living room and sat down on the couch. Fran came over and sat in the armchair, looking at him. Her hair was long and casually draped over her shoulders.

"How is your face?"

"It shouldn't scar, at least not badly. It's fine."

"Emotions run high."

"They do, Fran."

Silence. The clock above the faux fireplace ticked away the seconds. Fran's phone buzzed. It was probably Jack, sending a text to her from the pub, where by now he'd have run into his abnormally drunk father.

"Is that Jack?"

"It might be."

"Please Fran. You need to do the right thing." He took a deep breath. He wasn't making eye contact but looking at some point beyond her, letting her outline blur. "Leave Jack and don't tell him a thing. And talk to Alistair. Talk to him. You can call him on this number."

He stood up to leave and handed her a card he'd taken from his pocket. "I'm sorry that we had to meet like this. I'll see myself out."

She didn't stir. He walked out, shoes heavy on the carpet. The door shut behind him, the lock clicking, and Fran started to cry, very quietly, hugging herself tightly.

4

It had been a difficult year for Fran. She'd just felt weaker and weaker as the days had gone on. Dull grey day after dull grey day, with the same routine, getting up in the morning into a blank canvas with no paint. She'd always been confident and driven; it was something new to her to feel this bad. She'd get to the office and find that a job she once relished was now painful and a tightly-drawn cord around her neck. She talked to herself, wrote diary entries; one thing was certain, that she was no longer full of the conviction that she had done the right thing. She'd fashioned her life from the belief that she was right to have her baby, right to choose to bring him up and work, right to not want to go to university, take a professional career, right to fashion her own path on her own terms.

It was Sean, her son.

He was strong, independent and funny and she knew she'd done a good job in bringing him up to be questioning and self-reliant. Recently, though, she couldn't look at him without thinking of Alistair. It wasn't that she wanted Alistair, or that she pined for some enquiry or attempt at contact. These things didn't matter. It was that Sean had never had a father figure. He'd never even had a stand in, Fran had never had a relationship of enough depth for that to happen.

There was one man, who became a friend who called round for coffee and biscuits, with the remains of a love affair like long-expired ash embers under their feet. The room was messy with the past but they put up with it. And Sean had grown to like him, the feeling was mutual, but he was heading out of their lives, not into them. And that was years ago.

Sean never complained but she felt more and more hurt and couldn't understand why. He wasn't asking for anything at all but she felt more and angry that Alistair had never once been curious; not about her – that didn't matter – but about his child. Every day it became more apparent to her that what she wanted was Alistair to answer for what he'd done, because he never had. There was a divided set of train tracks that formed her and Sean's life that felt as if they were meandering back to union. Gradients and the play of the geography and the lay of the land were engineering a new decision for her. Either that, or it was all in her head.

She went to the gym and ran as far as she could on the machines, pumping the iron up and down on the press benches. But nothing alleviated the grim feeling of lead weights on her shoulders and back. Morning felt stale and used. She went to the doctors, who after a brief conversation and very little consultation, put her on a list to see a therapist. He prescribed anti-depressants. She'd yet to see the therapist.

They were small pills that she took once a day, with water, at the prescribed time, another routine to add to the others. It was routine that had worn her away. It was the routine that was pressing down on her, comfortable, dependable and fashioned on things that were fragile and illusory. But she carried on.

5

Jack came back from the pub fairly late. He didn't have a key to Fran's but had arranged beforehand to come around after his drinks. He knocked out a pattern with a beat missing and Fran could tell he'd had a few. She went to the door and opened it, startled a little by his presence so near to her, so immediate. Jack walked in and hugged her, waited for the usual *how was it* or *did you have fun?* Neither came.

Her hands were awkward around his frame. Her timbre changed as she felt the circumstances shift. Fran felt her voice choke in her throat and she let go of him, turning and walking to the couch where she sat down. Jack immediately sobered up a notch, sensing that something was amiss.

"Fran, is everything okay?"

"Yes, why wouldn't it be?" She was looking up at him in his jacket, which he began to take off and hung up on a pine coat stand in the corner of the room.

"No reason. Dad was as drunk as I've seen him in years. He was completely random. I tried to catch up but he was pretty far gone. He said he'd had a massive business lunch. A liquid lunch more like." When he turned, Fran had her head in her hands, her hair cascading over them.

"Fran?"

She was silent. She pulled her hair back over her shoulders

as she re-established eye-contact. Her eyes were red and puffy.

"We should talk, Jack. There's something that – that you need to know." Something in her tone was sharp and brutal. He didn't try to argue, sitting down in the armchair and paying close attention to her. The room swam a little as he tried to focus.

"Okay. Go ahead." He was preparing himself for some sort of revelatory speech, something along the lines of, "you're too young, I'm too old." Pints of Kronenburg had made him a little woozy and anaesthetised. It all seemed a little like a game at that point.

"Well, I had a visit today, Jack. A visit that moved some things into quite clear focus." She took a deep breath. "I had a visit from Ray Baxbury."

She waited for Jack to compute. His brow creased and he asked quietly, "How do you know Ray?"

"I've known Ray a long time, Jack."

Jack's mind raced into the inevitable conclusion. His face retained its inquisitive aspect.

"No…"

"There is no other way of saying this and there is no tactful way of telling you, but when I was very young, I lived in the town that your father and Ray used to… 'party' in." She watched to see if he was following, and his eyes were suddenly sharp and focussed, looking directly into hers. "I was young and I started a relationship with your father, Jack."

His eyes became blank and uncomprehending. The clock seemed to slow down, stop, or at least every other sound in the world faded down to nothing. The only sounds that existed to him were his breathing, her breathing and the sound of her voice. She waited for him to interrupt but he appeared to be entering some sort of shock. She carried on.

"I had an affair with your father, Alistair Wilson. It lasted a few months, Jack. And I got pregnant, with his child. I kept it. I have a son by him called Sean."

Jack's face seemed drained and pallid. He struggled to look at her as he had done, his head swimming, racing. He worked out her child's relationship to him. He imagined a scene in lurid Technicolor, his father on top of the woman he'd confessed love for just a few days ago.

Jack stood up, drunkenly, almost losing his balance. His eyes were wild, lost, obscene and unfocussed. He ran to the toilet, pushing open the door with enough force so that it struck the wall and slammed back into him, hitting his face flush. Fumbling, he pushed it again and Fran heard the sound of him being sick into the toilet.

Jack vomited again and again into the toilet and finally slumped down, his back against the radiator, his legs bent underneath him, his head tilted back at forty-five degrees. He closed his eyes and pictured himself shaking some hands, smiling gratuitously. As hard as he could manage, he shut his eyes tightly.

Fran didn't move from the sofa. There was nowhere to go to, not a single thing that she could say to Jack. Minutes passed, where the ticking of the clock faded back into both of their lives.

At these points you can keep on talking. The voice becomes a paintbrush, adding the strokes and finishing the detail. Each word is something more, another shred of evidence and shard of pain. Words add up alongside words to wall in the conversation.

Fran could have spent all night talking, and detailing, and Jack could have spent another lifetime asking her why in different shades of grey. All of them would be mixed on a palette of incredulity. He could have asked her why and why not and the whether it was this or if it was that; deep and long and dark and long into the broken night they'd trade blows, until, like two tired heavyweight boxers, they'd clasp each other in round fifteen, spent.

They both sat still and said nothing. Jack stayed in the bathroom, his stomach cramped up and his knees up against his chest, tears managing somehow to slide down his cheeks even though he wasn't crying. Her stark confession was implanted in his mind. After around ten minutes he started to cry and carried on until he was choking.

After five minutes of hearing Jack in the bathroom, Fran stood up and put on his coat. She shut the door quietly behind her, intent on finding Alistair.

6

The world that Fran found herself in was one of conflicting signs. It was months before she actually turned up at Shore's that she had come up with the idea of going to find Alistair in London. It went against 20 years of silence and non-contact, so the impulses that made her want to do it led her to ask deep and sincere questions of herself.

The self-medication was chilled white wine on nights in alone, a pad of paper and some hastily scrawled diagrams and notes. 'Why are you doing this to yourself, to the both of you?' she'd write. Underneath was a blank page, until the first glass was gone and the wine stem still cold and cloudy with condensation. Her lipstick made a red smudge at several points along the rim.

The world of conflicting signs now amounted to a pad of paper and fountain pen with the ink drying in the nib. The lid lay separated from its body and master, covered by a ball of screwed up A5, the edges visibly ripped out of the notebook. The wine was cold, the air was cold and she felt cold. The beauty of her youth was fading into the half-suppressed sob of middle-aged regret, and that was something she couldn't allow. She couldn't stop ageing but she wanted to do so without the frantic scrabble of nails on smooth glass, at the window of a bus as the stops fly by, rain-lit pavements reflecting the lights back up into view.

Her vision would swim as she finished the bottle. What she wanted was for Alistair to be a man about the whole thing. He'd never been a man about any of it and it rankled with her. The father of her child was a love cheat and a selfish, arrogant figure of disdain. Others might say in real terms the father amounted to little more than a sperm donor 20 years ago. But that's how the passage of time had left her feeling. She took a pill out of the box of 30 and put it into her mouth, letting it linger a while before she washed it down with a gulp of wine.

"There's nothing I want," she said as she lay back and curled into a ball on the couch, the only sounds from the clock on the wall and the heating pipes, trapped air clanging round and round. "Nothing I want."

7

Fran shut the door to the block of flats behind her and heard it click. The night air was cold. She dug into her pocket for her phone and pulled it out. The message from Jack she'd received earlier was still unread. She clicked it up. 'Dad is pretty drunk. Will be here a while but will come back soon. Jx'.

In her other hand she held the card that Ray had given her. The coat she had on smelled of Jack, of his aftershave and perspiration, of roll up cigarettes and the Tube. She took a deep breath as she typed the number, taking a few more steps out of the front enclosure and onto the street. Turning left, she walked toward the Tube station. Hitting the call button, she looked up at the horizon and caught a glimpse of Canary Wharf, its light ever-blinking. The phone rang three times and then a voice picked up.

"Hello. Alistair Wilson speaking. Who is this?"

Fran didn't say anything at first, but then spoke, firmly. "It's Francesca, Alistair. Ray said I should call you."

His voice shifted as began to answer, but soon returned to the officious tone he'd answered in. "Yes… I'll be with you in a few seconds." She heard him move through whatever building he was in. She guessed he was moving to a place where his wife wouldn't have a chance of overhearing.

Perhaps he had been in bed with her? Talking tenderly as she changed into her nightgown in front of a full-length dress mirror. A hairbrush, a compact, a dusting of powder.

She heard feet on steps. After ten or so seconds, he spoke again. "Okay," he said. "I'm glad you called. I was in the kitchen, sorry." He was lying. "I gather Ray came to see you today."

"He did, yes."

"You talked?"

"We talked."

"Would you like to talk things through with me? Did Ray spell out what we thought... What we thought the best course of action would be?" He sounded business-like, in the register of a man taking a call about a troublesome contract. She paused and thought about what she should say next. His tone of voice irritated her. "I just told your son about us. He's in pieces."

There was breathing at the other end of the line. He inhaled; cleared his throat. A crackle as reception dipped down and then the line cleared.

"You – did – what?" His voice was strained but barely above a whisper.

"I told Jack about you and I at your wonderful parties back when." She made her voice steel, cutting through his formality and his attempt to handle her like a stock transaction.

"I – asked you... Ray asked you not to. What have you *done*? ... Did you think of Jack? Revenge on me is all very well but," he now shouted, "did you think about what this would do to my *son*?"

"You don't care about what it does to him. You care about what it does to you. And I'm going to stick around to see what it does do, until you acknowledge both your *sons*, Alistair Wilson."

She clicked off her phone and carried on walking, counting the seconds until this proud and arrogant man rang back on his knees. It took eight. She took the call and repeated her dictum.

"Listen Fran, this is ridiculous –"

"Did you hear me? Until you acknowledge your *sons*, Alistair."

"We need to meet. This needs to be done face-to-face, okay?"

"I don't know that it does."

"I would like to talk to you, Francesca."

"You want to talk to *me*?" She laughed. "That's nice. It's taken a while for us to get to this stage, hasn't it?"

"I didn't see you ring me."

"I had no intention of ringing for myself. This is for Sean, my son. There's nothing I particularly want from you for myself."

"We really need to talk this through in person, Fran."

Her heels clicked on the pavement. She was coming to the end of the street, a crossing, and now stood next to some traffic lights and a pedestrian crossing. People lined up beside her. Cars started to drown out her conversation.

"Okay."

"I'll text the address of my office to this phone. Where are you now?"

"I'm near Aldgate Tube Station."

"I'll be able to meet you in forty minutes, at the address I'm going to send to you."

She thought about it for a few moments. "Okay."

"I'll speak to you in a while." He clicked off. The lights changed and people started to cross, so she did too, taken by the crowd. There was a pub on the corner that she went into, walking to the bar. The radio was playing Alanis Morrisette.

No-one was waiting to be served, the barman idly tapping the bar in time. He took her order, a glass of white wine. She took out some money and he asked small or large; she nodded noncommittally. He poured a large measure. She gave him a five-pound note, and he handed her some small change. The track changed.

She cast her eyes over the clientele of suits and office workers in semi-casual. The corner table was unoccupied. In her pocket, she felt the phone buzz once with a text message. As she sat down it vibrated again. She took it out and took a sip of the wine, a sip that turned into a gulp.

'Where have you gone (and with my coat)?' asked Jack. At least he was functioning again. Her heart fluttered and tears came to her eyes at the thought of the pain he was going through. She loved him back; she'd said so. She thought she felt something. But what did she understand by 'love'? She took a huge gulp of wine again. A tear made it through and slid down her cheek. No-one in the pub noticed. The next message was an address. She'd get the Tube, meet him in half-an-hour, maybe make him wait. She didn't reply to either message.

Memories were coming back to her. She was young and passionate and Alistair was a tall and handsome lion-tamer, with effortless command over others. He smiled at her and she wanted to be his. They'd gotten drunk, intimate, pressure of flesh on flesh. She had been young and stupid. She'd even hoped that she'd get pregnant. She'd spoke idly over cock-tails at the weekend that she was already done with school and didn't want any of it. She looked back at those thoughts and thought about how young she was. It was an impossible, precious undiscoverable stupidity that lay glazed beneath a sheer surface; always the surface of things.

She wanted to feel something different. She wanted to feel

that she owned something of *him*. His flashlight smile. The natural authority. He was married, so what? He wanted her, naturally. She was precocious, smart and sassy and turning into a woman right before him.

It was a house of cards, a tall tower of lies. The lies that we tell ourselves are the ones that hurt that most; that much she'd been told and told over by her mother. She believed it now more than ever.

Her mother and father's face as she walked out on them, her father pressing for them to go to the police, pointlessly angry in his idiotic vest; her mother crying and sobbing, and Fran's heart iced over. A mother at sixteen, she came back home. She saw a glimpse of her own face in the mirror at home as a woman of twenty-five, deciding finally to raise him with nothing to do with the past. She'd lied to herself even then.

Her wine was done. Each empty glass a happiness and sadness in one. She stepped out into a light drizzle and headed into the station, her feet slightly slipping on the stairs. The air felt thicker down here, laden with dust, history, charged with electricity. She gathered her paper ticket in her hands and put it through the machine. It popped up, out, proud, others waving themselves through with cards bleeping on the machine readers.

She took the Circle Line to Liverpool Street, the train arriving with a creaking moan. It clattered into the station. A girl got off in front of where Fran was waiting, her hair and clothes styled to perfection, her body thin and toned. She gave Fran a diffident, uninterested glance and then pulled a phone from her bag. Fran wanted to push her over and stamp on her, but instead got on the train and sat down, waiting for it to make its slow way through the maze of track junctions and traffic lights. It shuddered off and then jolted back as the driver's pilot light went out – someone pushing the door open or maybe their bag stuck in one, having bolted from the stairs to the train. Slowing to stop, the driver tried again and it moved off.

"Would passengers please not obstruct the doors? Thank you," said the driver, heavily, a male with a broad Essex Estuary accent.

Fran closed her eyes and took a deep breath. She had no idea what she would say to Alistair. She'd not really practiced this at all. She'd told Sean that was going to stay with some friends in London, and left him to get on with his life for a while. She thought of his endearingly messy flat, his laid back attitude, and his piercing eyes. She was proud of her son in a way she was proud of nothing else. He'd not said much when she'd left with a heavy suitcase, reading her signs. What must he have been thinking when she left? Her suitcase with wheels. A symbol of movement. Movement and fixity both. She guessed not much because Sean would have felt it rather than thought it. Unlike Jack, who played the analyst, quizzing his way through life.

She closed her eyes for what felt like a few seconds but was longer. The train pulled into Liverpool Street and she changed, going down the escalators after crossing platforms. The air grew hotter still; the commuters changed dress, changed colour, changed hue. London's microcosm.

The train to Holborn came quickly, sweeping into the platform at speed. The carriages were smaller and hotter than those on the Circle Line. She managed to get a seat again and after scanning those around; closed her eyes. They pulled off quickly and the noise soon overwhelmed everything else, dry and stale air rushing into the carriages from the tunnels.

The seats were set lower so she was a little more comfortable. She felt tension in her muscles. She was jolted back and forth. Her mind felt tightly wound, like a coil, around a magnet. The rattling beat of the train on the tracks soothed her. It stopped at the various stations along the line, a mechanical female voice making sure that Fran didn't forget where she was. Its piercing volume set her on edge.

As the train pulled into Holborn, she got up and unsteadily made her way to the door as the driver hit the brakes particularly hard.

'This is Holborn; change here for the Piccadilly Line,' said the well-spoken electronic woman.

Fran got off the train and headed up to street level, out onto Kingsway and round to High Holborn. There was a little drizzle in the air, not really worth an umbrella but wet enough to start making her face damp. Her hair quickly clumped into strands. The road stretched out in front of her, all the way to Chancery Lane. She turned down a side road and made her way to the address that Alistair had given, following his directions in the long text message.

She took a right, walked down a narrow street and then a left. The rain suddenly kicked in, falling harder. She didn't have any way of keeping it from making her wet. After a few minutes, she was close. When she reached her destination, she found Alistair waiting outside the office, under a large umbrella.

It had been over two decades since she'd seen him. And so the expectation, the recognition. A few steps took her closer to him and he held out his canopy of an umbrella, covering them both easily. The rain pattered onto the canvas; they looked at each other wordlessly.

He was older by degrees, sternness in his face that hadn't been there before. He looked at her. She looked at him. An exchange of half-thought out intentions. His hair was salt and pepper grey, cut short and fashionably, combed into a neat side-parting. Hers was long, draped over her shoulders, some of it haphazardly caught in her collar where she'd thrown Jack's jacket on. He recognised it as his son's after a few seconds, his face giving it away. Eventually, after around a half a minute, he spoke.

"Shall we go up to my office?"

"Yes, let's do that," she said.

They went passed a bored looking security guard who recognised Alistair, but then returned to whatever he was watching on the screen beneath the desk. Alistair pressed a button to call the lift, closed the umbrella. They were all parked on the ground floor; one of them pinged into action and the doors slid open. Once inside, he jabbed a button and the doors closed with a thump.

'Going ... up,' said a mechanical voice, a lady. It was a chorus of made-up voices in turn making up her day. The atmosphere in the lift was one that was hard to place. She'd never intended to come back; he thought that this woman was gone from his life. She was shorter than him and she turned to look up, eyes concentrating on his face. He turned to respond, the lift large and spacious. He might have been about to say something when it slowed and the doors slashed open to present them with a well-appointed lobby, leading to an unmanned reception.

He walked past it and jabbed a code into the door, an electronic lock releasing it to his already waiting hand. They marched through an office with the usual pot plants and cubicles, to an office with drawn-blinds against the windows. His door was locked; she thought of it as a slight overkill. He typed in another code and it opened.

The office was fairly large and minimalist, with a coffee machine in the corner by a little sink, some artwork on the walls, a large desk and a leather executive chair. It was as she would have pictured it. It was almost a send-up. Two less formal chairs stood opposite, and he motioned for her to sit down on one. He went to his desk and pulled two tumblers out of a draw. Towards the other side of the office was a cabinet that seemed to have some whisky in it, together with other bottles of spirits.

"I thought we might use a drink, under the circumstances. It might help oil the wheels."

"Do you have any ice?"

"There's an ice-making machine, yes. It's in the little fridge that the coffee machine sits on." Her eyes followed down to what seemed like another cabinet but was obviously a nice hardwood frontage for a mini-fridge. It was the office of a spoilt executive, the minimalism hiding toys and luxuries that the rest of the office would have to share, if they had them at all. She sighed.

"Go ahead, then. I trust you'll take care of the details."

He went about getting some ice, crossing the office and for a while standing outside of her line of vision. She caught his lean silhouette in the glass behind his chair. He gave her a small, folded flannel from one of the drawers and passed it her. She dried her face. He eventually sat down and pushed a tumbler towards her, adding a carefully measured shot of whisky to it.

"I really don't know where to start," he said. "It's been such a long time." He paused and looked her, remembered more clearly the danger that she posed to his life as it stood. "We might, I guess, start with the news you imparted to me on the phone."

"We can start there."

He was silent, then: "You've told Jack about me and you, then?"

"Yes. I told him just now."

"What I'd like to know is, why? Especially after your talk with Ray. I thought he explained."

"He talked, that was all. He explained nothing. Did he tell you I slapped the arrogance off his face?"

Alistair leaned in. "No. He didn't tell me that bit."

"You've not seen him this evening, then? After his visit?"

"I went home after seeing Jack."

"You missed it, then. It would be coming up as a lovely bruise, about now." She heard her voice, harsh, grating, and hardly recognised it. She took a sip of whisky. It was smooth.

"We're not here to talk about Ray. I'm here to ask you a simple question. I'd like to know why you came back, and why you are seeing *Jack*." He was starting to seethe with anger as he delivered the final line.

"I went through this with Ray, but I guess we'll have to go through it twice."

"This isn't something to get flippant about, Francesca. You came back, that I can vaguely understand. You might want something from me and you might have suddenly – bizarrely after all this time – felt aggrieved. But now I find out that in some sick and twisted perversion, you're sleeping with my son?"

She resented the tone and his anger, self-evident in his hectoring. He continued. "You're sleeping with your son's brother."

"He's no relation of mine, you fool!" she said, exploding at Alistair. "He made me think of *you*, Alistair. Who you were. Who you were before you ran back to your *lies*."

"I hardly call a successful and lasting marriage and a lucrative career a lie, Fran. *You* were the dalliance. It was a few months of illicit sex."

Old wounds, re-opened. She was still and very quiet as she examined his face; he looked right back at her.

"Now, you know that what you've just said isn't true, Alistair."

"I asked to you get rid of that child."

"Supposedly in my best interests."

"Supposedly? You were sixteen, intelligent and beautiful. You had your whole life ahead of you. Men would have fallen at your feet."

"I was fifteen, Alistair, and you were breaking the law with a minor. And you were never held responsible for what you did."

"What I did? What *I* did? I wanted the easy way out for us both and I wanted to make amends to you any way that I could. Being a father to that child, Fran, and leaving my wife were not options I was considering."

"So you said."

"And so I still say!" His voice rose. He took his glass and a large sip of whisky.

"Look at me, Alistair. And look at what she is now."

"You've never even seen a picture of her."

"Look at me."

"I don't have to look at you. I need you to clear out of this mess and, please, for decency's sake, get out of Jack's life. What future does he see, with a woman no doubt unable to have children and clinging onto the last bloom of her beauty?"

She couldn't contain her anger at his jibe. He'd worn down any grace she may have had towards him. He was strange, cold and not the witty man she'd been magnetically drawn to. Had she lied to herself back then? She had always thought her thinking was so clear.

"I'm going to tell your wife about us, because of what you've just said. You, you are a spiteful, withered old man."

He tried calling her bluff. "Would she believe a woman

like you? In turn, you are a spiteful, withered *middle-aged* woman. You're a delusionist with a crush on a man of power, Francesca. That's how she would see it. You're some client who fell for me. Just picture it."

"You always wanted to leave her. To take me. You just weren't strong enough."

"We had a few months in the sun, Fran. Were you suffering from heatstroke? We were sloppy a few times and you got pregnant."

"You wanted that baby as much as I did, Alistair. You've not stopped lying to yourself in twenty years. You *loved* me."

"I did no such thing," he said, without pausing.

"Yes, you did."

"You were a child back then; what they hell did you know about love and understanding, and what I could possibly have wanted?"

"I understood you. You knew that from the second you met me."

"You were an amazingly well-developed girl with a good line in party chat."

"Why would you have come down a day earlier than Ray, just to take me for a drive? And to make me food and sit. Watch the sun go down? You think I've forgotten? I wanted you to stand up and admit something we both knew was true and you sold me out."

"Sold... *who* out? You were a... *mistake*, Fran! I should never have gone near you!"

"You're a liar!"

"You're a madwoman with your claws in my *son*! How the fuck would I have managed to live a life with you? The shame, the scandal, the eyes. Everywhere, the dirty looks. My friends would hardly have wanted you at their fucking parties, Fran."

"And you cared for those parties? You did no such thing. You never have done, admit it."

"My wife is a wonderful woman."

"You spent your twenties cheating on her, until you met me. What changed, Alistair? Did I put you back on the straight and narrow?"

"I grew up."

"How many women did you fuck after me? Look at yourself. You… have been in love with me since we met, Alistair." She stood up. "You have been in love with me and you regret what happened every day; you have *dried up* inside. You can't look at Jack sometimes, because you see your other son. He's called Sean. I called your son Sean. But you try not to think of the child you had with me. You can't bear that I never called, begging; you can't bear that I lived my life and brought up my son and that I never came looking for you. You can't bear not being needed. You have to be loved, cherished, at all times. That I have loved and loved fully since you, you can't bear that in any woman. That I never looked back for your hand in mine. That Sean is beautiful and strong and nothing like you, you sad, old, emotional cripple –"

"Enough, Fran –"

"You can't bear that I didn't dance to your tune, get rid of the baby, carry on being your lover. That was the deal breaker and you called the deal off, and you've missed me your *whole fucking life* –"

"ENOUGH!" shouted Alistair, getting up and hurling his empty tumbler at the wall. It sailed past Fran's head, a velocity of magnitude, and shattered on the wall behind her, glass splintering in different and random directions. She was stunned into silence.

Alastair was red-faced and he looked at her, earnestly. He took a deep breath and came out from behind his desk. He walked up to her until he was close to her. She could smell the whisky on his breath. She could feel his anger as short, ragged breaths. He was showing stubble shadow and looked tired. He came still closer and looked directly into her eyes.

"I need you to go back to whichever rock you crawled out from, Francesca. No more confessions. No more damaging the way things currently are. Just go."

She waited. She said nothing, and waited. She moved her head up, tilting it back. She looked at him, eyes wide. There was nothing but the tick of an expensive clock on the wall, the hum of the refrigerator and the sound of their respective breathing.

He moved in to kiss her. She met his lips for a second, then took a step back and slapped him across the face.

"Too... late!" she said, tears flowing down her face, a hand into his cheek to break up the words. "Too fucking late, Alistair. Twenty years too late." She left him, standing there stunned, as she moved towards the door. Opening it, she picked up a business card from the top of a cabinet next to the door.

"Do you know what I want, Alistair?"

"What... do... you want?" he said, taking his hand from his face and resting both of them on his hips, one thumb tucked into his belt.

"I want you to acknowledge to the world that you are Sean's father. And that is *all* I want from you. You... pathetic... husk of a man." She was dragging out the words and then she left, slamming the door.

Alistair sat down in his chair, heavily. The clock ticked. He pulled her whisky glass towards him, looking at the lipstick stains on the glass. The bottle was still out and he topped it up, halfway, more, whisky dribbling down the rim onto the blotter pad.

She'd not told him in so many words. She'd missed a period, she'd told him that much. One day, he lit a cigarette and passed her a glass of champagne, a Friday before another heavy weekend of parties and revelry. She put down some LP or other and looked at him; they'd had a connection. She hadn't taken the champagne flute. He knew what she wanted to say, often without her saying it at all. His reaction that day had made her cry. He looked shocked, pale, had put both glasses down on the sideboard and opened the patio door. He walked out of the room, onto the beach, and he hadn't come back inside for a long time. She had waited as patiently as a doll.

"You have to get rid of it," he'd said when he came back in.

Her hands had been gripping the LP so tightly that she snapped it when he'd said that. He could hear the crack now, only now it had deeper relevance. It was the crack in his own life.

He'd always hated the way that this young girl had been so right at every turn. She'd been right about what he wanted to do, about how he felt at the time, about his friends. She'd make remarks about them when it was just the two of them in the kitchen smashing ice with a club hammer, and he'd laugh and laugh.

He knew, deep down, that she was right now. He knew that she'd tell everyone, that there was no way she would stop after a few words in an office. He drank what was in her tumbler. He poured some more. A weakness, seeking solace at the bottom of a glass. He was a father twice over. He was a father of two sons.

The office was so quiet at that time of night, emptied of action and of intent. He leaned back in his chair and felt a wave of tiredness. He'd never felt that tired as a young man. It was tiredness in his very centre that felt as if it would take him with it over some precipice. He got his phone out of his pocket and bought up Ray's number. It started to ring as he pressed the call button.

"Ray."

"Alistair? Heard anything yet?"

"I've just spoken to Fran. She was in my office."

"Oh," he said. "She called you much more quickly than I thought she would."

"She's…" he started to say and then tailed off. He exhaled and looked round his office. He was sick of those paintings.

"She's told Jack. We had a row. She said I was still in love with her. And she's going to tell Rachel unless I admit to everyone in some sort of bloody family conference that I have another child by another woman the same age as my own son."

Ray didn't say anything.

"Do you want to meet tomorrow morning? We should talk this through a bit more. Not now, though. I'm quite tired. I think I might… sleep here."

"That's not a good idea, Al. Get home to Rachel and get some sleep."

"She said some cutting things, Ray."

"She is – a cutting woman. Get some sleep buddy. I'll see you tomorrow morning."

"Okay." He clicked off.

Alistair dialled for a cab as he left the building. There was music playing, somewhere, in the night.

Part III

1

Jack eventually got up and left Fran's bathroom. His knees felt weak and the world swam around slightly as he took his first step. The edges of his vision crackled. The lounge seemed a huge distance away but he got to the island of the couch and sat down, breathing out in a sigh. He looked up and saw the coat rack. His coat was missing. Fran must had taken it to wherever she had gone to.

Jack fumbled in his pocket for his phone and some random phrases tumbled into his mind. Anxious not to say just any-thing and certain of the fact that he would, he put it back, looked around again and counted the cost of the last few hours. He couldn't fix his thoughts at all; they were just ran-dom things that bordered on shapes of emotion and shades of meaning. Relenting, he sent a text message to Fran and then regretted it instantly. The clock seemed to have stopped as he got up and tried to make a coffee, his hands shaking with the effort, his body refusing to behave.

Ray was gathering his thoughts over a glass of vodka and tonic, in his kitchen, the television blaring through from the unoccupied lounge, doors left open, the house lights up and bright. His wife came down the stairs. It wasn't late, but she'd had a nap. She'd mentioned something about work being hard when she'd come back earlier and had gone straight upstairs, not even popping in to check on him, see that the side of his face was cut and swollen, bruised purple. He'd been sitting in his armchair with one of the nested tables pulled up close, his hand around a can of lager, the coasters left stacked up. A condensation ring had slowly formed on the table. As she breezed past now, smelling of a shower and her favourite perfume, hair tied up in a towel, he felt decades of memory solidified, calcified and sedimentary in the way they had accumulated. She flicked a switch on the kettle and turned, then stopped as she saw his face.

"What... happened to you, Ray?"

"Nothing. I fell over at work; it was a bit stupid of me. Landed flat on my face, can you believe it?"

She looked at him, then down at the drink. She knew this man, better than anyone else. So many years had passed between them that she knew there was something wrong.

"You... fell over at work? That doesn't happen usually."

"No, someone left something out, some junior idiot. A file on the floor or something, I didn't see it. I should get him sacked for this." He attempted a smile but he couldn't. The events of the past few hours had stirred something up inside of him that he was struggling to deal with.

She looked beyond him at the open door, the television on some nonsense channel. She looked back but didn't want an argument. The kettle was rumbling deeply, the steam building. Finally, it clicked off and she spun round on her heel, movements proud and disdainful, a half spoken "huh" choked down before it had been vocalised. She quickly got a mug from the cupboard and a teabag from the box they were kept in, grabbing the kettle with a heavy hand and sloshing the water in, spilling a little as she focussed so hard, thinking about Ray but determined to keep the thoughts as low-level radio interference.

Elizabeth was always determined to triumph in situations like these. Ray's easy demeanour concealed a temper; Liz concealed a steel determination to keep her emotions tightly reigned. She knew Ray was lying, but his lies had stopped hurting her, at least superficially. It was just a few paces to the fridge to get the milk but, as she made each one, she felt her defence slip. These latest few years with Ray had began to change her. She was so tired.

"You're lying to me," she said, as she held the carton of milk in her right hand.

"I'm… not lying to you, Liz. It happened at work." His face was blank and drawn.

"You're lying to me!" she said, considering hurling the milk at him. She stopped short, pulling her arm before it tensed too hard. She turned and put the milk back, the expensive fridge clunking shut with the thick sound of the rubber seal on the metal. She hadn't put the milk in her tea, though. She'd have to go through the process again. As she stood there, considering, Ray got up, grabbed his drink, ice clinking with the motion. He went into the lounge and shut the door. She carried on making her tea, stirring it a little harder than she had to and throwing the used spoon into the sink so that it rattled around before it finally settled.

Jack had made his coffee. He brought it to his lips and took a sip. It was hot, strong and it took his mind off his stomach, still tight and cramped up at the thought of what Fran had told him. She'd slept with his father. He had a half-brother by her. Earlier today, he'd spent a few idle minutes wrestling with the age question, was she too old, where would it ever lead?

Would he be able to have any children with her if it got that far? He'd teased out suggestions and half-solutions in the gaps that made up his working day.

Now it wasn't about that at all. It was concerned with things like the fact Jack's father wasn't just his father. And in no way was he the man that Jack thought he was. He tried to fathom the duplicity, the years of accumulated lies. His mind changed tack: he couldn't let his mother find out. If Fran had told him, who else would she tell? Panicked, he looked around the kitchen, as if the room itself would offer up a solution or a clue. Had Fran gotten with him because of a chance meeting or was this more calculated? How could it not have been more calculated, considering the history? His eyes continued to scan the walls but there was nothing forthcoming. It was the same silence as before, with no respite from the feeling of suction, of loss, in his lower abdomen.

When had he last felt this way? He tried to remember, tried hard to push through the fug of the day's events and get to a comparative state. He wanted to set down a marker, to return to himself. Who had he become in the last few minutes, slumped and tearful on a rug in a badly-decorated bathroom? He'd become who he was heading towards being. That future was becoming his present, here in a flat not his own, with the evening turning into the night.

Elizabeth pushed open the door to the lounge and saw Ray sat in his armchair, his hand pressed up to his face, leaning into it. The television was on but he wasn't watching it. He was just following the shapes and the sounds as he slowly slipped into a drunken reverie. She walked up to him and sat on the couch, facing the armchair, her gown still on, hair still up, holding a mug of tea by the handle and resting it on the material covering her knee.

"Ray, we have to talk."

"I know we do."

"How much longer can we go on like this, Raymond?"

He didn't reply. She looked at him a little more directly and straightened her back slightly.

"If you can't talk about us, at least tell me the truth about what happened to your face."

He pondered what he might say. That a girl Alistair Wilson had gotten pregnant over twenty years ago was back in town demanding that he acknowledge his illegitimate son, and that Ray was trying to keep it all quiet and had gotten caught in a fight that really wasn't his own? Elizabeth might find out that he'd slept with Fran too, but it was before he had got together with her, when Ray had been single.

He was trying to hold onto someone else's secret. He wanted, he realised, to protect Jack. But he was so tired and Elizabeth was so trying when she questioned him, over and over. She'd invariably not let this drop until he gave an answer that satisfied her. Was their marriage over? He looked at her and tried to feel how he had felt all of the years he had held that woman's hand and woken up next to her. He didn't want her to leave him. The last few months had been terrible, a never ending succession of arguments and heated rows, cold war in the bedroom and a few soulless couplings, almost for continuity's sake. Why was this it, he asked himself? Why should it have gotten so bad?

"Do you really want to know, Liz?" he said, languorously.

"Yes, I do."

"Will you come and sit down here?" He patted the arm of the armchair.

"How irregular," she said, suppressing a smile. She sat down and he could smell her near him.

"Do you remember when I was younger, that I spent a lot

of time with Al, at the Beach House? Most weekends, in fact, for a while. Did I tell you?"

"You've told me some of it. I dread to think of the rest."

"I got up to a fair bit, yes. But all before I met you, as you know."

"As far I've been told."

Ray put his arm around Elizabeth's waist. "Well, this cut doesn't concern what I did, so much. It concerns something that Alistair did. Something that's suddenly re-appeared. And it is a problem that I've been trying to help him contain, as much for Jack's sake as Al's. But I am the one who caught the crossfire, so to speak."

"Okay. Go on." She was sat above him, looking down, noticing the finger-shaped bruises on his cheek.

"Well, it went a little weird for a while. Alistair was going up earlier than I was to the Beach House and coming back later. It was when I only knew you as a friend. We'd been on one date, I think. You kept telling me to get lost, actually. Anyway, he had a woman. Another woman."

"So," she said, languorously, "this was when he was with Rachel?"

"I'm afraid so, yes."

"The male code, I see. You kept his infidelities quiet. Has he returned the favour?" She pierced him with an acute gaze.

"I've never cheated on you, Elizabeth," he said. "Not once."

Some time passed as she gauged his tone, his timbre, the pitch and tilt of his voice. She nodded for him to continue.

"This girl was one of a few over the years before Jack was born. But in any case, I think she turned out to be a little special, in terms of what they felt for each other. It was all a bit intense... I don't really need to go into the specifics. She was called Francesca."

"A sordid little secret, then? "

"I – well. Anyway, look." He paused and thought about how best to say what he was about to say. Like he'd done with Alistair just a few days earlier, he decided to come out and say it with a blunt force.

"He got Francesca pregnant. She was fifteen. She kept the baby, Liz. And he's pretty much the same age as Jack."

"Oh my – " said Liz, covering her mouth with her hands. She was silent for a long time, looking at a distant point with her eyes drifting over objects in the room. The coffee table, with its austere lines, was piled up with magazines. The *objet d'art* in the corner on a wooden plinth was in stark contrast to Ray's assorted junk on the oak desk next to it.

"I haven't finished."

"Well, go on then," she said, still sat on the arm of the arm-chair, but with that sentence stood up, pulled a footstool over and sat across from him.

"Francesca left, kept the baby and never really bothered anyone. She was proud and loved the baby by all accounts and raised it by herself, I assume with her parents help. We basically heard nothing after that summer, and Al stopped renting the Beach House. They closed up shop. A little town; I think that's what happens, maybe. I don't know. She never challenged Alistair over it – she asked him to leave Rachel and he didn't, and they just never spoke again. Until now."

"What do you mean? She's *here*?"

"She's come to London, yes. And she was looking for Alistair, but – oh fuck me, this just gets worse and worse. It sounds incredulous. She was looking for Alistair but met Jack and they – got together."

"What?" said Liz, her anger rising. "This is a wind-up, Ray. This is disgusting. You're a deeply unfunny man some-times."

"It's not a lie. She was with him, but it's all gone belly up; she wants Alistair to acknowledge her son, she's told Jack and she's going to tell Rachel, and it's all a mess, and oh – I just. Fuck. I just don't know." Ray tailed off and put his head in his hands. He exhaled, slowly, and tried to look Liz in the eye, but couldn't. She was sat there looking shocked. He carried on looking on the floor.

"I'm appalled, Ray. At this, at what he's done, at the fucking *lies*. The twenty year lies and hypocrisy and betrayal. And you *knew*! I feel sick, Ray." She stopped talking to take a breath and pierced him with her steel gaze. She was a formidable woman. He knew the strength she had to cut him out, leave him cold. "I've been living with a man who would protect a lie for a friend even though there are children at stake, lives that have been buried from public knowledge. Jack has a half-brother! With this – his *girlfriend*? I need a drink." She got up and headed over to the drinks cabinet.

"This is sick," she muttered, as she poured a measure of brandy into a crystal tumbler. She took a deep sip and then turned back to face Ray, who was ashen-faced and seemed to be on the verge of tears.

"What are you going to do, Ray?" Liz asked.

"I have no idea, darling. This isn't my fight, but Jack's distraught and if Rachel finds out, it will end his marriage."

"It should end ours, Ray. Do I *know* you anymore?"

Ray had no idea what to say. He'd been expecting her anger and the last few months had been dismal with regards to their actual marriage, but never thought that this concealment for Alistair would be the final weight, a stone that tipped the scales. He looked at her for a long time. She was scowling, a drink in hand, ready to shout at him again once she'd formulated her phrases.

He'd first met her at some event or other. He was young;

she was younger than him by a year. He'd been speaking to someone about something, bored and holding a full glass of white wine. She was impossibly arresting, piercing eyes and a great, strong bone structure. He went over, said hello and asked where she was from and if she thought the art was up to much.

"I didn't come for the art. I came for the canapés and the free wine. What are you doing here?"

He'd loved that line so much. He laughed, they spoke, he was single, so was she, and he asked her if he could call her sometime. He did and took her to Reviens for dinner, where he made a fuss of her and she was non-plussed. He tried harder and she still didn't budge. Finally, exasperated, on the fourth date, he took her hand in his and spun her round on the walk home.

"I want to kiss you, Elizabeth."

"Tough," she said. "I don't want to kiss you."

"Why not?" he said, taken aback. He thought the date had gone well and the wine had flowed.

"Because there's a strange man over there looking at us, Ray. Maybe… we should go back to mine?"

"For the kiss?"

"For a drink, I meant. I'm still not kissing you. Even there"

"Ha. Well, lead on."

They argued over it and, eventually, she did kiss him, he stayed round, and he knew that he'd marry her after just a few weeks. They'd gotten on well in life, professionally, and she'd kept at her career. They'd never had children. They had tried and found it hard to conceive; they thought about fertility checks and treatment, but they didn't see the rush. Soon, it was too late; Ray took Jack on as a surrogate. It was too late and had they ever really spoken about it being too late? He pictured punching a ball into the air in a park. The noise of a cricket bat, leather on willow. A child to call our own. A fascination with birth, ideas of succession, shin pads in the hallway and ruffling a buzz cut with calloused hand. He looked at her now and thought about what kind of a mother she would have been.

Was it really over? Was there no love left?

"I don't know if you're in the right frame of mind to be talking about our relationship," he said, leaving his reverie, trying to address the present.

"I don't think you have much of a say considering what I've just heard."

"All of that has nothing to do with us."

"How can I be with a man who would lie like that?"

"Was it my truth to tell? Was it my responsibility? What right did I have to tell people and break apart a marriage, see my friends divorce, see Jack's parents split? I am not one to interfere."

"You never even told me, Ray!"

"You would have been straight over there. With your righteous anger and indignation. You'd never have left it alone."

"Right, so you don't credit me with a brain."

"You've just said yourself I was some sort of reprobate for keeping the secret. I knew because I was there, but their marriage has lasted; I'm not going to be the one to tell them about some pointless affair twenty years ago. She should never have kept that baby."

"How do you have the authority to speak of these things? Are you a father?"

"That's not fair, Elizabeth."

"Jack sees you as slightly roguish uncle, Ray, that's all. Don't pretend that you're the authority on what is right for families."

"That is enough," he said, sternly.

"You think you know so much – what is it that makes you so wise?"

"I don't think I'm wise, Liz, but at least I'm not always shouting my mouth off about things I know fuck all about."

"Really? Has it come to this? Swearing at me in my dressing-gown? As we trade blows about the child we never had and the lies you helped to protect… about other people's children that should, according to you, have never been *born*?"

"Liz, please."

"Ray, just go." It sounded like the snapping of a heavy but old piece of wood.

Ray visibly crumpled in his seat, then looked up, eyes asking the questions. Her face was set hard. He looked at his desk for re-assurance, things, a random accretion of paperweights and pointlessly expensive pens. Was that his life? Or was this his life, here, held in his hands, his marriage stale and his wife accusatory? What he needed was distance from it, perspective to put it all into order.

He stood up, a little unsteadily after the large measures. The emotional state he was in was distinctly uncomfortable. He viewed his feelings as friends whose love had passed into anonymous approval and general disregard. He had no time for them when they had no time to make him feel good, to support him. But if asked to name how he felt, he was unable to. He wanted his thick leather jacket and a pint, to walk around some town centre with a pal and find a pub. What was it, inviting amnesia and numbness. A parade of absence. He looked around the room, the collection of objects, the clock on the wall that was five minutes fast. On the mantelpiece were pictures of Liz and him, smiling, on holiday with friends.

"I'll go then. Something has to be done. Something." He walked out of the room and began to pack upstairs, haphazardly.

Elizabeth came up and approached him from behind, putting her arms around his waist and hugging him tightly.

"Maybe we just need perspective, Ray."

"I know, I know. I'm sorry."

"I love you, Raymond."

"I love you too, Elizabeth." He turned round to face her.

"I have loved you since I met you at that terrible private view, Ray," she said. "It's just, you've let me down."

"Maybe."

"I always wanted to believe that you'd have told me something of that magnitude."

"Whatever I did, people were going to get hurt. It was a difficult choice to make. I wanted to protect Jack."

"I know that you had his best interests at heart."

"I'll stay at a friends for the night. I'll call you tomorrow about where I'll being staying after that."

They looked at each other, the passage of years still funnelling back to that night at the view, eyes locked over a piece of loaded bruschetta, the fabric of their lives pulled taught.

2

Jack looked at his mobile while he was sat in his room. The large display was clear and crisp. As he hit a button, it came to life, glowing in the mid-afternoon dark of his room. The curtains were drawn and he'd taken the day off work. He felt sick, tired and unhappy. He lay back on his bed and stared at the ceiling for a long time before reaching out for the phone and tapping a few keys. He bought up Fran's number and pressed dial. Jack didn't expect her to pick up but, after three rings, she did.

"What do you want, Jack?" she asked. Her voice was stern, crackling.

"I… wanted to talk to you."

"We're talking."

"I wanted to ask you… if we could meet, to talk in person." He left the sentence hanging, his voice unsure, his sentiments vague, imprecise.

"I don't think that's a good idea," she said, cringing herself at the sheer banality of the phrase.

"Right," said Jack. He let some seconds pass and heard her breathe gently into the mouthpiece. He missed the sound of her breathing next to him, though it hadn't been for long. It was a quiet and shallow breathing, the rhythmic rise and fall of her chest.

"Is that the end of the conversation? I think we've said all we have to say."

"We really haven't, Fran." He felt his insides spasm with the intensity of his disappointment, but he tried to keep it from his voice. It was a struggle. "I think," he continued, "that we have a lot more that we should talk about."

"Like what, Jack?"

"I know you made out you were someone, when in fact you were someone else. And that you'd had a relationship with my father. But isn't that all in the past?" He knew he sounded ridiculous and desperate. "I just want you. I just wanted you."

"You just want me? You want to *wipe the slate clean*? You want to forget about your half-brother that you have... through *me*?"

"Why did you start anything with me – you knew, you knew who I was, Fran? Why did you do this? Why did you do this to *me*, of all people? What the fuck did I do to you?" Asking for answers after the fact had struck Jack as a protracted analysis of the ashes.

"I worked it out soon after. But I admit Jack that I did fall for you, very deeply."

He reacted to the confession with a sense of renewed optimism, tinged with the knowledge that what had come out over the past few days had already, irrevocably, damaged things.

"If you fell for me deeply, you'll want me again." It wasn't a question; the cadence was dispirited and ended almost silently.

"I do want you, Jack. But this can never be. And I have to make sure of this."

"You're shutting me out on principle."

"No. Just listen to what I say next, very carefully Jack."

She gathered her thoughts and he pushed the phone into his ear a little harder, then readjusted with the resulting discomfort.

"I want your father to acknowledge his son because he got away with what he did for far too long. And I am going to tell your mother about me and him, about Sean."

"You – can't. You really, just… can't," said Jack, choking on the words. "No, just don't."

"I want to."

"Why?" he asked. "Out of malice? What good can this confession of Dad's achieve now, after all these years?"

"Closure."

"For you?"

"For everyone. Why should the secrets stay secret? Why should he have won and held onto everything he held dear?"

"And you haven't had these thoughts before? In your decades living your own life away from all this? Why now?"

"I think I had a very strong resolve, Jack. But it has slowly been broken down. When I met you, all the old feelings were brought back. I don't know what I felt before. I felt nothing for years. In the end I think it was you."

"You're pinning this on *me*?" he asked, exasperated.

"In a way, you were the catalyst. I came to London with an agenda, but you turned it into a certainty."

"Catalysts remain unaffected, *unchanged*, Fran. I am most definitely… Fucking. Changed. I'm changed and I'm… so *sad* at what you want to do." He let the rancour take hold, the hatred of the power she had over him and the hurt she had afflicted.

"Whatever you are, Jack, you are a part of a family that held onto is integrity despite the misdemeanours of its father. I wasn't the only one. And I am sure he knows much more than he has ever let on. Look at yourself and look at if you want to end up like him, Jack. Look at me and walk away. Let your father pay."

"I'm – unwilling to do that."

"You're unable to walk away from something you want, Jack. But you have to be stronger than that. You have to take this from me, Jack, please – be a stronger, better man than your father was. You have it in you."

"You don't know me. You've just proven that I don't know you either."

"I know you are a better version of him."

"He's achieved a lot, whatever you say about him. And from the sounds of it you came to London with the express intention of destroying my family."

"At what cost have his achievements come? At what price to you? To your mother? How well do you really know your father?"

"The family stayed together. That much is important. You're preparing to break it apart." Jack felt bitter and his voice was raised.

"Well, you know now. And Alistair most certainly knows. Why leave your mother out? Would it be fair to let her go on and on through her marriage and her life without possession of the pertinent facts?"

"Are you a barrister now?"

"Jack, I'm ending this conversation for your own good."

"Fran, please. Think about this."

"No, Jack. Just – get some rest. And... I'm... I'm sorry," she said, after a long pause where her voice was near to breaking. He didn't say anything in return and, after a few seconds, she put the phone down. He put his head down on the pillow and turned over on his side.

Across London, his father picked up a phone in his office. He dialled a number, about to make a business call. Just as the dial tone caught, he hung up and put the phone back down. There was so much to think about. Leaning back, he put his hands behind his head and exhaled. He thought about the past few days. He thought mostly about Fran's threat to tell Rachel about their affair. He tried to visualise the damage it would cause; in its simplest terms, she would ask for a divorce. Would she take him through the courts? No doubt she would.

He tried to picture a life without her, back to living in a bachelor pad and making regular maintenance payments. Watching her move someone else into his house; or maybe she'd sell it for the money, now that Jack had moved out. Watching the house itself fall into disrepair as it was neglected. He pictured hanging out in bars trying to catch the attention of a woman, making moves at a club or over a drink at a pub. He pictured dating. He could barely remember what he was supposed to do. Ray on one side, a man struggling with his middle-age the way a toddler struggles with a complicated toy. The slowing down that comes with the ageing, the intense hangovers, the mornings where nothing feels right at all.

There was a knock on the door and he put his hands back down on the desk, said "come in". It was an assistant bringing in papers for him to sign. He'd seen them before so looked over them briefly and distractedly signed them. She gave them back and turned to go, revealing an amazing figure and a pencil skirt draped over impressive curves. He pictured him and her briefly for a minute, all erect cock, flesh, sweat and disregard. He laughed at himself. Who did he think he was, and what was this? He couldn't think about it like that. He wasn't able to think of anything in any way at all. Vague shapes of emotion.

After she'd left and shut the door behind her, he stood up

and walked the short distance over to the filing cabinet. For a long time, he found that he had stood with hands placed against the varnished wood as if it would bring relief to all of his problems.

Fran was sat in a brightly-lit room, the sunshine streaming in through the open window, the curtains pulled back and the net curtains tied up in knots. Before her on the coffee table was a mug of tea, steaming into the air. There was a fabric to life that had its own weight, its own sound, she thought. The gentle cadence of her mother talking her to sleep at night made her want to cry because her mother was old now, in a nursing home somewhere on the South coast. The tinkle of wind-chimes would forever take her back to her childhood garden and the preciousness that was engendered in one so young by something that she still couldn't put her finger on. The lullaby that had gotten to her bed that one night with the thunder and the lightening was long passed into the soil and the earth, a sound wave still faintly reverberating in its weak and degraded state, memory a mirror to past glory.

Fran picked up the phone and called her friend Tony.

"Hi Tony, it's Fran. I need you get me an ex-directory number, if you can."

"Hi Fran. I'll give it a go, sure; what do you need it for?"

"I just need to talk to someone I haven't spoken to in a while. Her number's not listed and, to be honest, I have no idea how to get it as its been so long."

"Right," he chuckled. "I know how it is, too proud to beg. What's the name?"

"Rachel Wilson, married to an Alistair Wilson, which will probably be the name on the bills."

"Just tapping into the old PC. How are you?"

"I'm good, Tony. How are you?"

"Same old. Pub and home, dinner for one. The microwave and me. You should come down and keep me company more."

"Ha, well, I think we both know what you want from that particular arrangement."

"Come on. I can be friends with women too."

"Maybe your mother, Tony. No-one else."

"Well, have it your way. I have a huge film collection. It's a shame more people don't get to enjoy it."

"How's the PC getting along?"

"Well, it's a slow one. But it looks like I have a few matches. Alistair Wilson, Hull?"

"No, is there another?"

"Quite a few more. Five more with a London postcode, two suburban. You want both?"

"Middle names on the bill?"

"This will cost you a visit at least, Fran."

"Okay, okay – a visit. I will come round at some point next month to watch a sodding film with you and no doubt drink a bottle of whisky."

"Good girl. Alistair John Wilson and an Alistair William Wilson."

She racked her brains and remembered a driver's licence. "William Wilson."

"The number is as follows. Got a pen?"

"Yep."

He read the number out and then, after a few more pleasantries, they ended the conversation. She looked down at the number she'd written and prepared to dial it.

Pausing, Fran realised she had no idea how Rachel Wilson would take the news. Would she acquiesce to the truth? Or would she protest her husband's innocence and refuse to listen. Would she even be home?

The dial tone rang. It rang four, five times and, just at the point where it might have switched to answer phone, a haughty voice answered, "Hullo? Wilson residence."

"Is this Rachel Wilson?"

"Yes, it is," she snapped, obviously out of breath having run for the phone. Fran pictured a large, expansive house and Rachel sitting drinking Assam tea in one of the rooms, a long way from the telephone.

"This is Francesca Darlington," said Fran. "I'd like to speak with Rachel Wilson about a matter of some importance."

"You would? Well go ahead. I have no clue what this is about. Are you sure you don't want Alistair? He's at work and I can pass his num –"

"No, its you that I'd like to speak to, Rachel."

"It's Mrs. Wilson to you. Go ahead." Fran heard her take a seat near the phone. There was a little interference on the line, a whoosh of crackling that cleared up as soon as it had arrived.

"Well, I am an acquaintance of Alistair's, Mrs. Wilson. I knew him well."

Rachel immediately grew very suspicious. "This had better not be some idiotic prank call; I just haven't the time."

"I was a partner of his, Mrs. Wilson. A sexual partner."

"I'm putting the phone down, Ms. Darlington, and I'd advise you to stop dreaming."

"Rachel, listen to me and drop the haughty housewife act. I am Francesca Darlington and I have some news to pass on to you. Are you listening?"

"Look, this – "

"I said, *are you listening*?"

The conversation stopped flat as Rachel re-adjusted her expectations of what it was going to lead to. This wasn't a telesales call after all, or another prank call from one of Jack's drunken friends, though Jack had moved out years ago.

There was silence. Rachel adjusted her necklace.

"I'll go on, then, Rachel. I presume that you are listening to me. I slept with Alistair when he used to come down to the Beach House at weekends. I'm sure you had some idea of what he might have gotten up to but, in any case, I am living evidence of his infidelity to you."

"I don't... believe you," said Rachel, slowly.

"You should. I really don't have anything to gain by admitting this, apart from a victory on principle for my son."

"*Son?*"

"I had a son with Alistair, Mrs. Wilson. I was fifteen-years-old, and it was just around the time that you were pregnant with Jack. I know, because he told me."

"This ..."

"... is incredulous? It is, I know it is. But I have no other reason for coming to London and telling you this apart from that I want Alistair to finally acknowledge his son and own up to what he has hidden for so many years. I... don't want money, or maintenance, or anything. And I know this will have come as a huge shock to you."

"A shock? A *shock!*" screamed Rachel. "How dare you call me and spin these lies, you fucking harpy! Damn it, who do you work for, who is paying you to say this utter bullshit? I'm hanging up – " said Rachel, and with that Francesca heard the first half-a-second of the noise of the weighty receiver being slammed down.

Fran waited a full ten minutes, drank her tea, which by now was starting to get cold. A skin had formed from the milk. The breeze came gusting through the window in bursts. She dialled again, because she knew that Rachel would still be sitting in the chair, staring at some distant point, pondering her words. The phone was answered quickly this time.

"Is this you again, damn it?" said Rachel.

"It's me. You have to ask yourself this, Rachel: if I don't want money, or anything at all, why would I lie? Where would I get to by saying this? What kind of sick fabrication would it be, being as I have nothing to win by it and that the onus on proof is on me. Do you want some proof?"

"How could you possibly give me proof?"

"Alistair's favourite colour is red. Back then, he was heavily into cocaine and would get nosebleeds from nowhere. He told me that he'd once gotten one in front of you in the General Forbes pub on Marlowe Street, in the presence not only of Ray, but one of your best friends who was out with you all for the first time in London. Why... would I know this Rachel, unless I had intimate knowledge of his comings and goings back then?"

"I... don't know," said Rachel, hesitating, falling flat on the last word.

"Here's another thing then. He has a birthmark just above his left knee, about ten centimetres up. It's basically on his thigh and shaped a bit like a oval."

"I've heard quite enough of this. Any of this could be hearsay and conjecture that you've heard in the company of his friends, and I really think that you need to end this call."

"What about this, then: he told me he proposed to you on one knee in the living room of your first house on Parker Street. The day before you'd had a row about the car you'd knocked into the lamppost and that you'd threatened to leave. He lost his balance as he went down on his knee and you burst out laughing. Now, why would I know all this, Rachel? *Why?*"

"Why are you doing this?"

"I have a family, too. My son."

"You have an illegitimate son that you claim is Alistair's. That is all you have. Please get off the phone. Goodbye."

She hung up and, somehow, Francesca knew that although Rachel had believed her, must have had to an extent, it wasn't the victory she had intended. She thought about if she wanted Rachel to cry, but no, she hadn't. It didn't feel like a conclusion. It didn't feel any closer to an ending. She didn't want to hurt Rachel. Who was Rachel to her anyway? A name, in an anecdote, a set of stories. A past narrative. She felt a deep confusion. Why was she doing this to someone who was ostensibly innocent? What had happened to turn her into this stranger to herself. She had possibly just ruined a marriage. She felt an incredibly heavy weight upon her shoulders.

Shutting the window with the hollow thump of plastic on plastic, she left her hand on the glass. Almost silently, her cup fell onto the carpet, tea spilling all around her. Outside, cars and people streamed by, oblivious to her dilemmas and her actions, her inactions and inabilities. The world went on while Francesca took her hand from the glass and lay down on the sofa, heavily, glazed, drained of the impulse to breathe and live, fearing for the future.

3

Sean Darlington woke up in a haze. His mouth felt dry and sticky, and he had trouble focussing on what was directly in front of him – the wardrobe across the room.

He gathered his thoughts and remembered as far back into the previous night as he could. A drink after work with a friend, which then turned into more drinks as other friends arrived. There was a shot of tequila at one point as someone congratulated him on something or other. A cocktail was introduced into the mix later on when a few girls arrived, one of them with a boyfriend in tow, who had been eager to please the assembled males with a show of prowess. And what better way than with a large round at the bar, buying his way into their hearts? They toasted one another and returned to the matter at hand. Forgetting exactly what they wanted to forget was high on the agenda.

His hangover pounded into his skull with every slight movement. He reached across to the bedside table and gathered his cigarettes and lighter. He took a moment to tap one out of the pack and then had a smoke, a long drag on a cigarette momentarily making him forget about the fact that it hurt to move. What time was it? It was Saturday, and it was 1pm. Steve, his closest drinking buddy, had been allocated the morning shift. On the table next to the cigarette pack was his mobile, with a message on it that had failed to wake him up when it had arrived.

'So much pain. Is it worth it?' It was from Steve, saved in his phone as Hawaii Steve-O after some particularly gruesome summer shirt wearing last year. He didn't find the joke funny anymore.

He didn't have the energy to even reply. He felt around his neck to make sure his necklace was still there. The blinds were drawn. He thought about his mother. She'd headed into London to 'go and see a few people' a few weeks ago. It had been maybe a fortnight. He'd not been too bothered about it. Her life was her life to live, but the cadences in her sentences weren't quite right. They hadn't been right for quite some time. Something about it didn't quite fit and Sean wanted quite badly to make sure his mother was okay. The sense of foreboding about her when she had decided to go made him feel insecure. There was a sense that she was going away to take care of something quite important. What could it be? He put out his cigarette.

He'd never once asked her about his father and that was the biggest grey area in his life. Other children had fathers but he had an empty void into which he dared not pry. Why would he? She had given him pretty much everything he'd ever wanted. She'd been a father to him as well as a mother. She'd been the one to take him to school on the first day and the one who'd turned up at The Owl on a Friday night to give him a lift home, dragging him away from the rumbling beginnings of another teenage fight.

The debt of generations is something spectacular. He tried to arrange the sentences in his head, but it seemed to be a day for doing nothing in particular. He'd maybe make a coffee, try to cook some breakfast, stumble around until he found the armchair, the remote, a good book, another desire to get him to the evening.

Something, however, was nagging him. He moved through the plans for the day in his mind, until going to London quickly materialised. He could check up on his mother. The major concern was that he'd not had word from for a week or so. The last message had been to check up on him – 'how are you? Eating well. Things going well, speak soon.'

He'd been drinking so much that week. He felt sick and tired. He had been drinking too much for years. Swinging his legs onto the floor, he stood up unsteadily, walked slowly to the kitchen. The coffee machine had some old grounds in it so he flicked a switch on the kettle and set about making a cup of tea. The was just a little bit of milk left at the bottom of the carton. The sink had some plates in it that needed washing up, the food dried on. London wasn't that far away. He could be there by early evening if he left soon and he could then check on Fran. She might need some support. There were people in London that he hadn't seen for a while too. They might want to go for a few drinks.

The thought of drinking made him feel a little ill, but he grabbed the cup of tea he'd just made and headed to the bedroom to pack a few things in a rucksack. He'd get on the train and be there before the evening. If his mother was in, he'd reassure her and then head off to meet some friends. It seemed simple.

The blue-black rucksack was fairly spacious even after he'd stuffed in a few t-shirts and pairs of jeans. He counted off the number of boxer shorts and socks he'd need, heading back down to the bathroom, to shower and then to collate his toiletries into the wash bag he'd gotten free with some after-shave several years ago. He replied to Steve while he was waiting for the bus. 'I don't know if it's worth it but we seem to have spent a long time finding out. SD.' His phone had a middle button that was starting to stick when he pressed it.

The train didn't take long. He was vaguely annoyed at some idiot sitting opposite him who blaring tinny music out of his phone. Relenting to the desire to redress the balance, he got out his portable mini-speakers, which produced a phenomenal amount of noise for their size. He fixed on the little table between them and switched on his MP3 player, drowning out the teenager's phone. The youth turned to look at him, indignant, but realised from Sean's blank facial expression that this wasn't a battle he was going to win.

"I thought you might like to listen to some real speakers," said Sean, leaning forward with an air of menace that the teenager misread as aggression.

"Get out ma face," he said.

"If you don't turn it off, I'll leave you with no real face to speak of," said Sean, looking around to see if the carriage was oblivious to their little altercation and then slipping a short flick-knife from his left inside pocket. "Just stay calm and turn that thing off, and so will I."

The youth looked back, ready to rise to the challenge, eventually thinking better of it. He collapsed back into his seat and switched off the phone. Sean reached down and turned off the music. He got some gum out and tossed the youngster a stick.

"Cherry and menthol," Sean said, returning to stare out of the window and watch the countryside fly by in a steady blur, which collapsed into a smudge at the furthest point of his vision. Try as he might, he couldn't follow the smudge. He rested his head against the cold glass and tried to get some sleep now that the youth was quiet.

The boy got off at the next station, the last local stop before the train shunted into another gear, speeding up and leaning into turns. Sean loved the idea of trains but hated the pungent, slow ones that he'd had to catch in England. He'd felt better gliding into some Central European terminus, stepping out after grabbing his rucksack from the overhead rail, arriving in a world of beer in small glasses and tasty-looking food. The sad sight of a baguette shop at an English train station selling two-pound cups of weak tea made his heart feel heavy and weak. He didn't want to become his granddad, moaning at the next wave of fashion he didn't understand and bemoaning the teenage argot that excluded him. Walking around at home in a vest. He felt around his neck to make sure his necklace was still there.

The train pulled into London, into the station, as trains do: a pause for the right platform, held at a red light; passengers being passengers pulled down their luggage too soon, shuffling around. A commotion to save a few seconds ensued. Sean let it pass him by, and the train juddered to a start, the industrial surroundings giving way to a sleek wall of steel, glass and a dozen platforms either side of the train. The driver announced that they were pulling in and the aisles filled with people getting in each other's way, frustration growing with every tentative and pointless half-step towards doors that would only open when the train stopped.

It took Sean a minute or so to acclimatise on the platform, but soon he spotted the symbol for the Tube. Hastily, he consulted a scribbled set of notes that his mother had dictated to him a few hours before she'd left. Which Tube stop, which direction from the Tube, and finally an address. He recognised the name of the Tube station and headed towards there.

Sean knocked on the door forty-five minutes or so later, but no-one answered. He dug into his left pocket and moved the cigarette case to one side, pulling out the spare Yale key he'd been given. The electronic card was attached and he used that to get past the main door, meeting a particularly stunning red head on her way out for a jog. He smiled at her and was given warm approval. She turned, about to launch into some final stretches.

"I'm here to visit my Mum; she's down in London for a bit. Off for a jog, then?"

"I'm more of a runner," she said. "I can't abide that lazy meandering around the park."

"Right," said Sean. "Well, she's up in Flat 6. I'll see you around."

"Flat 18, if you fancy a drink," she said, smiling. "Have a good evening." She turned away and broke into a slow run, accelerating after taking a right at the front gate. Women often reacted this way to Sean.

The key turned smoothly in the lock and the door opened. The lights were off and he made his way to the couch, putting his bag down by it. A small night-light was on in the kitchen. He walked towards it, switching on the lights. The flat was tidy and neat, as if Fran had deliberately just put everything away and in its right place. He went back into the living room and noticed a small pile of neatly folded shirts on the dining table. They weren't his. Why would she have his shirts with her anyway, he mused. He sat down, feeling worn by the journey. In his bag was a bottle of Diet Coke that he took a swig from. There didn't seem to be any ashtrays around.

"I'll just wait here," he said out-loud to no-one in particular. He took off his coat and placed it on a chair near the couch, sitting back down and shifting into a more comfortable position. He let himself drift off into a light sleep, his head nodding fairly soon. Tilting his head into the cushion, he soon drifted off to a deeper sleep.

This was how Fran found him an hour or so later, mouth open wide and breathing heavy and regular. He mumbled something as she came closer. What was he doing here? She'd made the phone call to Rachel Wilson that day. She was worse for wear after sitting in a small pub and drinking red wine until the pain engendered by what she'd done had faded. And now her son had landed in the middle of the mess she'd created ostensibly for his own benefit.

Had she lost her mind once she'd entered the M25? She could have told him first; maybe that would have been enough – if she had told him that his father was Alistair Wilson, that he had been older, had gone back to his wife, that they were fine. And that she was going to get Alistair to acknowledge him. But should she have let him have his say on what she did? She'd not consulted him, just been caught on one dizzying wave after another. She could have done it without the drama that now would no doubt ensure between her and her beautiful son.

She sat down in the chair that his coat was draped on. She smelt his aftershave. She'd definitely lost her mind walking into Shore's and meeting Jack Wilson. She was so far away from who she was. Where was her resolve? Had it really been worn down? Or was that an excuse for her selfish acts and desire to hurt, finally, after being hurt; even though, in the cold light of day, she had been complicit in adultery. Who was she to judge? She felt drunk. She was at sea.

"Mum?" said Sean, opening his eyes and wiping the back of his hand across his mouth. He stretched, sleepy but lithe. "How long have you been sitting there?" he asked.

"Not long, darling," she said, her voice quivering slightly.

"Are you okay? Are you… drunk?" he said.

"A little."

"What's the matter? You look like you've been crying." Her eyes were puffy.

She shook her head. "I'm fine," she said "I've just been out all day; it's tiring, and I'm tired."

"I know you a bit better than that, Mum. Even half-asleep." He rolled his shoulders to loosen them. "What's the matter?"

"I've just – I've made a bit of mess of things, Sean." She looked at him directly and held his gaze, saying it again without any hesitation. She let him know how serious it was.

"I'll… make you a coffee, then. You look like you could do with it. I certainly good. Can I smoke in here?"

"Yes."

"Okay, well, sit there, I'll be back."

He was in the kitchen for about five minutes working out how to use the coffee machine. There was the click of a lighter and the smell of fresh cigarette smoke wafted into the lounge.

"This is some fancy coffee," he said, across the rooms, raising his voice. "Where did you get it?"

"Somewhere in Covent Garden."

"Smells great, anyway. Be right there."

He returned with two milky Americano coffees and a cigarette clasped between his middle and index finger. He used a dirty cup as a makeshift ashtray.

"Is it something serious? I'm guessing – after thinking through the options at home today, and for the past week – that this concerns something from the past. Maybe even… my father?"

She turned to him instantaneously, almost with a jerk of sudden motion. Her face was blank. "What?" she asked.

"You were about to tell me what was wrong, in any case. And I'm guessing that I need not guess. Why don't you drink your coffee first though? Tell me what you've been up to, apart from working yourself into a state?"

"I've been seeing some friends, sightseeing, taking a break

like I said I was going to."

"That's not what you said," he added, laughing. "You said you were coming here to sort some stuff out."

"Yes, some stuff in my head, Sean. I've been doing a lot of thinking."

"About what, then? You might as well be honest with me, Mum. I can see through your falsehoods. And you know it." He smiled at her and then returned to carefully flicking his ash into the cup.

"It is to do with your father. I out-ed him," she said. "I exposed him, to his family, and to his wife." Then, just as she threatened to burst into tears, she held it back. "I should have told you first, but I didn't. I just came here and did it. I don't know why. It's such a mess."

Sean was silent and looked at her face for clues to how he should respond.

"I just had this notion running round my head for so long and it grew in size and stature; that this guy should say in public that he was your father, that it would please you and it would mean –"

"Mum, you're rambling. This – man's – admission would please me how?" He paused to look over at her and then said, "Look, go back to the start. You came to London. What did you come here for, exactly?"

"To meet with Alistair Wilson, your father."

"Alistair Wilson." He smiled. The idea of a father was faint joke to him. To him, his father hadn't really been much other than someone who provided the requisite sperm. He had whittled it down that far, in terms of what kind of credence he should give to the notion of a father in his life.

"I came here to talk to him and persuade him that he had to acknowledge you as his son. I thought that it should finally all be out in the open." She paused and nodded at him, as if that were supposed to spur him to add his input. He wondered when this had turned into a support group.

"How… long have you felt this way? Why didn't you tell me first? Anyone could have told you that it was a crazy idea."

She said nothing.

"Mum?"

"I… didn't speak to anyone."

"And you haven't spoken to anyone about it for years and years and this is what becomes of it. You didn't think about the damage a revelation like this would cause?"

"I *wanted* it to cause damage."

"And how does that help *me*? It just creates hurt."

"I wanted him to have to pay his debt to us!"

"What *kind of debt*? Money? You've never taken a penny from this so-called father. From all I can tell, you've never once contacted him. What was he supposed to pay? Pay his pound of flesh?"

"Why are you on his side?" she said, louder than before.

"I just don't know where my rational, strong and calculating mother has gone!" said Sean, raising his voice too and feeling a rising tide of what he might have called panic, had it not clearly been controlled and marshalled into his desire to leave there and go and knock on another door; find out that his real mother was staying in another room. "I just don't believe this," he said. He leaned into the sofa and lit another cigarette.

After about a minute had passed, she said, "I delayed closure for too long."

"Closure for you, yes! Just a name for me, Mum. Just a name and someone admitting to an affair with a young girl. Who have you *told*?"

Again she was silent.

"Who have you told?"

"His wife. His son. His friend knew already."

"Oh, man."

"It gets a lot worse. I... met his son first and... things kind of happened before I even knew where I was."

"This... really... couldn't get any more fucked up. You came here to what, totally fuck this family up? Wait – this guy is my half-brother? Fuck." Sean was silent for a long time. "You wanted to... leave his son in some sort of catatonic state when he realised who his new girlfriend was?"

"No. Stop this, Sean. Stop talking to me like this! I wanted Alistair to admit that he should have stayed with us! With us and not with his sham of a marriage! He should have stayed with *me*."

"This is so incredibly selfish. You've never been selfish, Mum. I just can't believe this has happened after all this time." He took a drag and exhaled. "After all this time, during which it could have happened anytime and it happens now, without a word to me and a hop, skip and jump to London to start a *landslide*. A fucking incestuous landslide."

They sat in silence, for a long time. Sean was feeling ill.

"Are you angry with me for wanting the truth to finally be heard, Sean?"

"This isn't you talking, Mum. This is someone who's hidden her feelings for too long. It's just all tumbling out, isn't it?"

Sean knew his mother so well. Her lip trembled and she put her hand over her mouth. Her head lowered.

"I don't know who I am anymore, Sean," she said. "I thought I knew exactly what I was doing... I don't know."

He moved over and hugged her. She collapsed into him, her strength failing. "He should have loved me, Sean," she whispered. "Those were the rules I set myself." She was talking into his shirt sleeve. "I wanted him to admit to having you. To not lie to his wife anymore. Why should he have gotten away with it, just because I was strong enough to keep my mouth shut?" She pushed back against his grip and looked up at him. "Because I was strong enough to keep silent and not talk? Is that why you don't know your father? Because I was silent?"

"Mum," said Sean, hugging her tighter. "Just be quiet for now. You need to sleep. We'll talk about this in the morning, okay?"

He tried to lull her into calm. He had no idea how long she'd been in this state, over-thinking, over-reaching. So those were the shirts he'd seen on the table. They must have been Alistair Wilson's other son. His half-brother, of sorts. He shared a father with someone then. Of the questions that were cascading in his mind, the idea of a brother, of whatever kind, rang most clearly.

What kind of trouble had his mum created here? She began to sob lightly – and she'd cried maybe once, twice in his presence, his whole life. She sounded desperately tired and ill. This was some situation. He tried not to think about what she'd gotten into. He tried to think about the next cup of coffee.

"I want you to have a father like the other boys," she said, crying into his chest.

4

"You lied to me," said Rachel to Alistair, who was stood across the room, arms folded. "All this time and you've been hiding not just an affair, but hiding the fact that you had a *child* with another woman." She ran her hand through her hair. "How could you do this?"

He didn't reply. She'd been talking at him for around ten minutes now. After five minutes she'd sat down at the dining table, at the other end of which he'd placed his hand onto it for support.

"You should just leave, Alistair. Just go. I want a divorce."

"Do I not get to defend myself, then?"

"You admitted what she said was true. The things she said, you must have told them to her. I just can't bear thinking about it right now. I want you to go."

Alistair paused for a long time. He stood up, stretched a little, facing away from Rachel. The boiler switched on. Water pumped in pipes. In the distance, someone let off a firework. Eventually, he turned to face his wife.

"This is my house, paid for with my money, Rachel. If you want to leave, be me guest."

"What? What are you talking about?"

"This isn't a house full of bouncing children and a mother they depend on, Rachel. It's me... and you. The mortgage is in my name. This is my house. If one of us leaves, it will be you. So, do you want to talk about this, or was that ultimatum your final word?"

His impassiveness got to her. He was stood, aloof, hands now on his sides. She started to cry, light sobs at first but then it cascaded into full, wracking, heaves. He still stood there, unsure what to do. Finally, he walked towards her, reaching her after a few steps.

Putting his hand on her arm, she reacted by batting him away and shouting, "I want my boy! I want Jack! Just call him. I can't bear the sight of you, you fuck. Alistair fucking Wilson."

"What can he add to this, Rachel? What can he say?"

"I want my son, you bastard! I need him here now," she shouted through tears, her words unclear through the sobbing. Alistair turned and slowly walked towards the phone. Rachel had grown steadily more frantic during their conversation, especially when he hadn't denied her accusations. What was the point in denial, he had thought. After Fran's detailed phone call, it seemed churlish to try and argue out of this when she could just call again, with more. Rachel had probably wanted him to denounce this as some girl who had a crush on him, to denounce it as lies; but, to both of them, they plainly weren't lies. The story of the proposal was one that Alistair had hardly ever told anyone. It seemed a little bizarre that it was unravelling after all this time.

His shoes made a clear and distinct noise on the floorboards. It was his house. It would remain his house. Rachel wouldn't force him out. He lived there.

"Jack?" said Alistair into the receiver.

"Yes?"

"It's your mother. She's… found out. Or rather, been told. About *everything*."

"Oh... fuck," said Jack, his words high and breathy.

"I think you should... come around. She's asking for you."

"What have you said to her?"

"I admitted to it. It doesn't seem to be worth it to continue to lie."

"How noble," said Jack sarcastically.

"I'd like to talk to you too, son."

"To impart some wisdom?"

"No," said Alistair. "I'd like to try to give you some reasons. As far as I can."

"I don't think I'd buy them."

"I don't expect you to buy anything. I just would like the chance to talk to you. But your mother wants to speak to you."

"I'll get the train over, then."

"I'll send a cab, wait at home."

"I think –"

"Just – please. Wait there, and a cab will pick you up."

"Okay."

"I'll see you soon, Jack," said Alistair, hanging up.

Thirty minutes later, the cab pulled up and Jack got out. The fare was charged to an account, and the cab driver pulled away from the kerb, crunching into second gear just a few metres down the road. Jack looked down the driveway at his family house. He hadn't grown up here; they'd moved during his late-teens. He'd spent a few restless years there before university arrived to give him the now familiar freedoms and the unfamiliar new shackles.

His old bedroom was still kept for him, posters cut from music magazines stuck into the wall with Blu-tack and sellotape, a secret box fixed onto the underside of one of his drawers that housed his drugs and secret bits of paper. He'd kept the original scrap his girlfriend had written her number on, in pink glitter pen. She'd passed it across to him in a bar where Britpop was playing. It was probably something by Suede, glam guitars chiming with the garish colours of the drinks on the sticky tables.

Once in the house, he went through and found his parents sat in mute silence in the living room. His mother had obviously been crying quite hard. She looked up and beckoned him over. Jack went past without acknowledging his father, and remained standing up as Rachel locked her arms around his waist and sunk her face into his stomach. She took a deep breath, breathing in his smell.

"Jack, it's all gone so wrong," she said, words muffled.

"I know, I know," he said, putting his hands on her head. He pulled away from her embrace and then sank down into a crouch on his knees, face-to-face with his mother. He put his hands on her face. "It will be okay. We're all still okay, essentially."

"I want him to leave Jack, I can't stand his face around me; it's just …"

"I'll talk to him, Ma. I need you to go and lie down, please."

"I just –"

"There's no rationalising at the moment. Just go upstairs and lie down. I'll talk to Dad. I will talk to him." Rachel nodded and stood up, heading upstairs, taking a route where she wouldn't have to go past Alistair. She walked slowly and deliberately, but in a few seconds was on the stairs.

Jack stood in the room and watched her, then listened out for her steps on the stairs. After a long time, stood with his hands on his hips, he turned to face Alistair.

"This isn't going to get fixed any time soon, Dad."

"You think I don't know that? She wants me to leave."

"Maybe some space would be the best thing. You're a big advocate of space."

"This is my house. She can leave if she thinks the marriage is over."

"That's hardly the attitude that's going to *save* your marriage."

"No." He was silent for a long time. "No, it isn't. It isn't at all. What should I do?" said Alistair, sitting down at the dining table. He waved at Jack to sit down too. "Do you want a drink? I could do with a drink." He moved towards his drinks cabinet, a wooden framed glass object, replete with heavy tumblers. "A big drink."

"Okay, then. I'll have a vodka coke."

"I'll just go and get some ice." Alistair got up and walked towards the kitchen. Jack let his eyes wander over the room, changed very little since he had left. Heavy, solid wood furniture was the mainstay. His father was a show-off. There was a black, overstuffed leather couch and an easy chair in the corner where his father would sit and occasionally smoke a cigar, like some sort of remnant of a by-gone era.

Jack knew it was all pose. So much of it was about stance. His father didn't even like smoking. There were paintings on the walls in muted colours, most of them in dark black wooden frames. He didn't even like painted art all that much. A canvas by some semi-famous artist hung on the wall near the narrow but tall bookcase. There was a bigger one in Alistair's office; it held a mix and made concessions to his mother's tastes. Paperbacks with heavily creased spines wrestled for space with literary novels. Completing the room was a large fireplace, a coal-effect one that was in fact fired by some incredibly powerful gas burners. They never had it on, really – the central heating was modern and also powerful. It was all just stance; his father's stance.

Alistair came back in with some ice and began pouring drinks. Eventually, he set them down on coasters, returning to his original seat across the table from Jack.

"I realised over the past day or so that I owe you a lot in the way of explanation. I've been forced by recent events into doing a lot of thinking." Alistair sat looking into his glass. His contrition was like nails on a blackboard to Jack. "And I knew that not all of it will wash because I've not been that good a person. But everything that I did, I did because things were better left unsaid."

"Things only go unsaid for so long, Dad."

"This didn't have to come out. I have no idea what went wrong with Fran, but it's like she's self-destructing or something. It stayed quiet for so long I thought that it was gone."

"What do you think… about her and I?"

"I have no words, Jack. I know you must be feeling a little sick."

"I don't. I…" he began, but tailed off. "I don't even know what I feel myself."

"Well, at least… I don't know. Fuck." He sighed. After a while he half-heartedly raised his glass. "Cheers."

He held it up and flashed a rare, if rather troubled, smile. Jack held his up in return.

"I have no idea how I thought it would work out. She's double my age, nearly."

"She was nearly half-mine. It's not a pretty equation, son. It's just not."

"No."

They drank in silence. A large clock with a pendulum on the far wall chimed the hour.

"When she… when she told me she was pregnant, I knew that I'd made one mistake too many, Jack. I had your mother at home, devoted to me. And you were on the way. I just…

knew that the sensible thing for her was to get rid of the baby, walk away and go back to school; live her life. She was so young, Jack. I was an idiot, she was so young, and we both had this ridiculous dream, fostered by too much space and too much time to think."

"Her child... is the same *age as me?*" said Jack, taken aback.

"Pretty much to within the month, yes."

"This... really isn't getting any easier. At all."

"No, it's not. But I need to tell you these things."

"Well, go on, then, I guess," said Jack, a heavy hint of irony in his voice. They both drank, glasses clunking onto place mats.

"She accused me of loving her. Of not being strong enough to leave your mother when I knew that what I wanted was a life with this precocious firebrand of a teenager. What I wanted was a life with her."

"I see." Jack let his father talk, leaving the floor open.

"I... thought about it a long time. Today, yesterday. She was a girl who affected me in a way that maybe I've never come to terms with, son."

"Explain."

"She said I'd grown bitter because of it. That I'd had this thing sitting in my subconscious all this time."

"Is what she said true?" asked Jack.

"Some of it is, yes. I do love your mother so dearly. I really do."

"But?"

"Ever since I told her that I wanted her to get rid of it and wanted no contact with her, I've had these two parallel lives running in my head."

"And you entertained notions of both? For how long?"

"Not consciously. It was just that, it set up a window into

another world."

"A world where you left Mum and me for a teenage *slut*?"

"Jack, please."

"You are making this much, much worse. The least you could do is have the conviction of your choices. The least you could do is say you don't regret choosing us."

"I don't. I had to. It was the right thing to do." He paused. "But she chipped a crack into the ice, son... I'm so old." He paused and set the glass he was holding down onto the floor. "I'm just so old." Alistair put his face into his hands, elbows on the table.

Jack looked at him, and took a sip of his drink, losing respect for his father as the clock counted seconds on the wall.

5

The next day, Jack woke up in his room and decided that he needed to get away. The weight of so many things was pressing down on his skull. The constant thinking and turning things over was making him feel weak and tired. Struggling to get up and make a coffee, he made a small action plan. He'd still not returned to work. He had to do something before he needed a doctor's certificate and so he was going to pack, go back to work the next day, and book all of his remaining holiday in one large stretch. He had no idea where he'd go.

As he sat gathering some belongings into a flight case, Anne knocked on his door. He knew it was her by her knock, a soft, delicate sound that spoke volumes about the way she picked up a spoon, did the dishes, closed doors or put books back onto shelves.

"Anne?" he said, tone rising.

"Jack," she said, pushing the door open. "Why... are you packing?"

"I've had some fairly distressing events occur recently, so I'm going away for a while," said Jack, still folding a shirt on his bed.

"Do you want to talk?" she said.

Jack looked at her and noticed she'd had her hair cut. Her

face was beautifully framed by a short bob cut, a fringe adding a neat touch. He'd always found her pretty, but he had kept her at arms length. Did she like him? She wasn't seeing anyone else. She smiled at him a lot in the house, and he'd caught her looking at him sometimes. Then again, he'd caught himself looking at her. He went for brunettes, usually, dark and brooding, with a sense of reserve. Anne was red-headed and freckly, a button-nose and a girly laugh that was more nervous than assured. What would he do with her? Where could it ever go? He put the folded shirt into his flight case.

"It's far too complicated and too soon, Anne. Thanks though," he said, looking at her and smiling. She smiled back, a little unsure of herself.

"Should I get you a cup of tea, then, maybe?" She had a deeply caring side that appealed to him. It wasn't the forced gesture of someone who thought that it was the polite thing to do.

"Sure," he said, standing up and gesturing that he'd accompany her down to the kitchen. He followed her down the stairs and, as she turned at the bottom to head to the kitchen, he got a side-profile. Anne had a great figure, curves reigned into a jumper over a short top and some faded blue jeans. It was half-term and she was off work. She looked up at him and smiled coyly.

"Are you checking me out, Mr Wilson?"

"I'm just looking at your breasts, that's all, Anne. Lead on." He smiled at her, the banter helping him forget what he was thinking about. While she filled the kettle, he got two mugs out of the cupboard. He tried to pinpoint what was happening. Were they flirting? He had his mind on escape, rather than entanglement. The idea of something happening between him and Anne didn't really fill him with any kind of longing or excitement.

Jack tried to think of why that was, exactly. Perhaps he'd never really run with the idea. It was difficult to tell in this kitchen with a mind full of cotton wool, knees still wanting to relent. He pitched his back against the kitchen worktop and felt the handle of the cutlery draw pinch into his lower back. The steam from the kettle billowed around.

"It's a woman, Anne. And it has to do with my Dad, too. It's all very complicated."

She looked disconcerted. "I'm sorry to hear that."

She put one sugar in his tea, the spoon already nestling in the sugar bowl. She stirred it absent-mindedly. "I've heard Mickey talking about this woman. Francesca, was it?"

"Yes, Francesca."

"It didn't last long then?"

"It wasn't really ever going to work out. We think these things will. Maybe the price you pay for lust and desire is a healthy dose of realism."

"Pragmatism, not idealism," said Anne, looking down at the tea cups.

"As far as it goes, I guess that's a fair approach."

"Not very melodramatic, though," she said.

"I think melodrama is vastly overrated. I'm not going to stand here and break dishes into the sink for anyone," he said, spitting out the words.

"You don't want the big hearts and romance, then?" She looked up at him, big eyes looking for answers.

"I did. A long time ago."

"Jack," she laughed. "You're not an old man."

"This fucking fast food age has turned its young men into young old men. I feel as if I can't do anything at all without some ridiculous amount of analysis and, even then, its still nobody's fault when it goes wrong. Just mine. Because I put

G. S. Mattu

myself on the line. I did this to myself, right? No-one asked me to go out there and fuck strangers that weren't yet even friends."

He turned away from her and walked a couple of paces out into the middle of the kitchen. He shook his head sadly and sat down on the couch by the wall. She took the handles of both mugs and brought them over to the table in front of the couch, placing them down gently. She smiled at him and put her hand on his.

"Don't let the bitterness win."

He took her hand and looked at her. "It's not that easy."

"It's as easy as you make it. You want to picture it as uphill struggle where everyone is out to get you, then it will be. At least, as far as you see it."

"I don't believe you're saying this to me."

"Why?"

"Teaching hasn't made you cynical?"

"I do... struggle. Yes, I do. But if I let it become my life, what do I have to get up for? The thirty ungrateful kids shouting at me and throwing their rulers at each other? Or the thirty children who are the same as me and you and looking around frantically for something to believe in?"

"What should I cling to then, Anne? You tell me."

"I have no idea," she said, laughing. "At least, not enough of an idea to be able to tell you to do anything." She got up and moved around, taking some dried crockery from the rack and putting it in a cupboard. "I just don't like to see you sad."

He didn't reply. He grabbed his mug and cradled it in two hands; he blew on it to cool it down and took a sip.

"I don't know if I believe in love," said Jack.

"I don't know if I do either," she said.

They both drank tea. A car went past outside, slowing to

let another vehicle pass in a gap. The driver crunched the gearbox into reverse to make a bit more room. Jack winced and Anne laughed.

"It's not hard to push the clutch down all the way, is it?" he said, accusingly.

"I don't know how to drive."

"Have you had any lessons at all?"

"In London? Are you joking? It's slow-motion mayhem out there."

"Well, maybe I could teach you. I've been driving for long enough. We could get L plates and I could take to you a car park, or something."

"I've had enough lessons to be able to drive around a bit. It's just so busy. And you think I'd let you take me to a car park? Ha." She laughed and went to get some biscuits. All they had left were Hob-Nobs. She placed them strategically on a plate, brought them over and sat down next to him.

"Have a biscuit. Give you energy for your packing."

"You think I should get some space, then?"

"Well, I don't know if I believe that you can run from yourself or your problems. My parents always taught me that it was nigh on impossible."

"No, maybe not. But still. Some time away. From the problem here."

"Some time away," she concurred, with a nod. She looked at him, massive eyes wide open, and lips full. He was so close to her, sat on the couch, legs touching at the knee and just above. He was unable to resist and reached in to kiss her.

She returned the kiss, just briefly, before pulling away.

"No, no, Jack, this is a terrible idea." She looked up at him. "This is a rubbish idea," she said, getting up and straightening the legs of her jeans with her hands, standing above him.

He stayed sat down and let the fracture widen. The ice was broken. They were separating. He returned his eyes to his tea, and let her stand there, before she turned around and went upstairs. She'd been waiting for him to try again, but he hadn't. She was waiting for him to follow through on his convictions, but he hadn't. Finishing his tea, he went upstairs to pack the rest of his case.

Part IV

1

Jack lay on his bed, a medium-sized silver flight case beside him. He'd had it since a family holiday during his teens. There had been a copy of some business magazine or other of his father's lying around. He'd seen the case there, advertised, some well-suited traveller looking assured. A semi-clad female somewhere in the near distance. He was more pliable than he cared to admit.

He'd packed a few clothes and was preparing to go into work to book his holiday. He was running through lines in his head, stock responses to the stock questions. Reaching into his right pocket, he pulled out his phone and tapped the dial key, bringing up his recent calls. He had the notion that he should call Fran and say goodbye. His stomach still hurt when he thought of her, but less so than it had done days previously. He could see the arc of recovery and it filled him with some sense of optimism. The brief kiss with Anne's lay heavy on his lips. He could hear her in her room, playing some poorly chosen music and humming as she folded clothes.

"Hi," he said into the phone as Fran picked up.

"Hi," said a male voice in reply. Jack halted, unprepared.

The voice sounded like it belonged to someone of his own age. He couldn't place an accent without more conversation.

"Is… this Francesca's phone?" asked Jack.

"It is, yes. This is Sean Darlington, her son. And you… are coming up on this display as Jack."

"Jack…Wilson."

"Oh. *Jack*." Sean paused and took a deep breath, translated to Jack on the other end of the line as a crackle. "I see. You must be Alistair Wilson's son."

"I am."

"Are we related then?" asked Sean, matter-of-fact.

"I… don't know. We share the same father… That makes us – what, half-brothers?"

"Complicated by the fact you've been with my mother, Jack." Sean was deadpan and cutting in his delivery. "You've been a bad boy."

Jack was silent for a long time. The line crackled just slightly and then the reception picked back up. Phones and circularity. Still, he didn't speak. Finally, some words managed to tumble from his brain into his mouth. "I didn't… really intend on getting into this conversation. I guess – I had no idea you would pick up. I'd not really heard much about you. Anything, in fact."

"I came down to see how Mum was doing. She's not doing very well. She's actually asleep right now, and I'm in the flat."

"Mine's not doing so well, either, it appears."

"How is Alistair Wilson doing?" asked Sean, an accusation veiled.

"He has also seen better days. I think we're all a bit shook up."

"That's an understatement, surely. It seems like I've arrived at precisely the point it was all melting down."

"Where did you arrive from?"

"South of here. I'm not going to give you the license to trawl after my mother like a love sick puppy."

"I'm really not that kind of man, Sean."

"What kind of man are you then?"

"What kind of man are *you*?" Jack asked.

Sean didn't answer straight away. He laughed a little. Jack heard the rustle of keys and a lighter flick out a flame. He heard an exhalation.

"Perhaps... we should meet up? To find out what happens when you take the same father and two very different mothers?" said Sean.

It was Jack's turn to pause. This was moving quickly; it was surreal. "I don't know if that would be a good idea."

"It seems like the fuss is all about me," Sean said. "Father this, mother that, secrets here and there. Don't you want to meet up with the prime exponent of all of the trouble?"

"You'd be the prime result of the trouble, surely?"

"Ah, the wonders of a good education. A carefully chosen phrase here and there to brighten up the day." Sean took a drag of the cigarette and switched his phone between hands to free up his right. "I have a notepad and a pen in front of me, Jack. Mum will be fine tonight. She's fairly tranquilised on some Valium I got in. Do you want to meet or not?"

"I do, yes." Jack did feel eager to find out about Sean. "Wait, *Valium*?"

"She was honestly in a bad way. In some sort of meltdown. I think I'll be taking her to the doctor's soon to get some sort of help. I just don't think she was a well woman. Which might explain a fair bit. "

"Oh."

"Yes, I guess it throws your tryst into a new light." Sean paused and took a deep breath. "Well, where shall we meet?"

A slight delay while Jack computed the options and then thought of Fran in bed, sleeping heavily, under chemical influence. "How about the Princess Louise just off High Holborn."

"Time?"

"7:30."

"And you would be?"

"The tall bloke in a black three-quarter jacket and, um, probably black jeans, too. I have medium length brown hair."

"Good, good. A wide spectrum of colours. I have a leather bomber jacket and will probably be wearing... grey jeans. I'm currently sporting a crew cut. I'll see you there."

"Bye." The phone went dead. Jack held it to his ear. The room shifted as he turned over onto his side and looked out at the horizon his bed sheets made with the rest of the room. So this was the next phase. Anne's stereo shifted to Aretha Franklin, her music player on shuffle. He got up, steady and sure. Opening his door, he stepped into the hall, knocking once on Anne's, pushing it ajar. She came to it, taking the handle and pulling it open.

"Jack?"

He kissed her full on the lips, and put his hands around her waist, pulling her in to him.

"I should have done this when we first met, Anne," he said, as they drew to a stop.

"You're rebounding on me, Jack." She looked up at him, having to tilt her head back to make eye contact. "Don't do this to me. Please." Her eyes were filling with tears.

Jack looked away. Letting her go, he turned, and left the room, not stopping until he was downstairs. Where could he go? The house was a vast open desert. In the spare toilet, he sat down on the seat cover with the door locked and was in there until it was time to leave for the pub.

2

Jack trudged through crowds of people. Occasionally someone would jab a free sheet or a telecom card into his path and he'd have to swerve to avoid it. He tried to look menacing but how could he look menacing with a fifty-pound haircut and a pure wool jacket? He dug his hands into his pockets and turned right at the Kingsway pedestrian crossing, taking a left towards New Oxford Street.

The density of people thinned out slightly as he took steps towards the pub. As he reached the reconstructed grandeur of the Princess Louise, he spotted a man with a black leather jacket and grey jeans, smoking a cigarette. In his left hand was a black drink in a short tumbler. Jack approached him, taking his measure. High cheekbones, like his own. His hair was cut short, very nearly in a crop but spiked up haphazardly. His lips were fuller than Jack's, his eyes brown and deep. The jacket was fashionably cut and had a zipper fastening. His jeans had a few rips on them, faded with use. On his feet were a pair of slim white Adidas lace-up trainers. So far, par for the course.

"Would you be Sean Darlington?" Jack stopped a metre or so from the man in question as he asked this question.

"I am. Are you Jack Wilson, then?" Sean put out his hand after clamping his cigarette between his teeth. They shook hands. Sean took the cigarette and stubbed it out on a smoking bin near the door. "Pleased to meet you. The man in question. You look rather like I imagined. Nice jacket. Nice *hair*," he said, laughing, and Jack winced inside. He wasn't sure why. "Do you want to drink inside, or out?"

"Well, it's a little cold, but if you want to smoke?"

"Do you?"

"Occasionally."

"Not a good enough reason to stay outside. Let's go to the bar." Sean confidently led the way, and, oddly, Jack felt a bit at sea. So this was Sean. Fran's son. He followed and they navigated through the low doorways to a snug that was occupied by one solitary drinker and a few empty stools.

"Do you mind if we take these seats?" said Sean to the old man.

"Nah, go for it mate," he said. Sean pulled a stool out and Jack sat down on the other. They looked at each other for a few moments. Sean was slightly shorter than Jack, but more lithe. Jack offered to get some drinks and Sean nodded. "I'll have a Scotch and Coke, please. Diet Coke."

"Right," said Jack, heading to the bar and waiting to catch the attention of one of the bar staff. There was one bar lady working, and Jack caught her looking across at Sean. He tried to get her attention and duly she noticed him, heading straight over.

"Hiya. What can I get you?"

"A pint of lager, please. And a whisky. Um, Scotch, with Diet Coke."

She nodded and went to get the drink. At the optics, she turned around and he noticed she had a fine figure. He caught the top of a thong, which dipped down below her waistline. She turned around to catch him looking at her. She suppressed her reaction. Heading back to the bar to pour the pint, he asked her where she was from.

"I'm from Newcastle," she answered.

"Cool. Well, I'm Jack; pleased to meet you."

"Likewise," she answered. "I'm Charlotte. Lottie. Is that your friend?" She nodded over at Sean.

"Actually… my half-brother. We're meeting for the first time."

She looked back at him quizzically. "And you came to a pub?"

"We might as well oil the cogs, so to speak. It's neutral territory."

"Aye. Well, hope it goes well." They exchanged money.

Jack thought about why he'd spoken to the barmaid. Was it because she had caught him looking at her? Or that she had been looking over at Sean? He took the drinks in his hand and wandered back over to him, placing them down.

"Nice barmaid," said Sean.

"Yes."

"So, is this like, your regular haunt?"

"No. I don't live round here. I chose it because it was fairly central and looks the part."

"I see. So you won't mind if I try to get her number later, then?"

Jack paused and took the measure of Sean. Had he noticed Jack's attempt to ingratiate himself with the barmaid? He must have been watching.

"Not at all. I don't think I was her type."

"I think you're a bit too clean cut for our Charlotte."

"You were listening in?"

"No, I just caught a few words. And I'd already spoken to her. Earlier on." He smiled with a air of mischief.

They stopped at that and took a sip of their drinks. "Here's to our… meeting up?" said Jack, proposing a toast.

"Indeed. Here's to us sitting here and having a drink. It might be the only good thing that comes out of this sorry mess," said Sean. He'd already made headway into his drink and had left it half-empty.

"What... do you think we should discuss?" asked Jack. He was looking at Sean still, trying to spot any kind of familial resemblance. They both had Alistair's nose. It was hard to take in; he had no comparative experience to place this against. He was meeting a man with whom he shared he father, a man that he didn't know existed until just a few days ago. And here this man was, in front of him, Dad's dirty little secret, raised away from the wealth that Alistair had given to Jack and Rachel. Raised by a single mother, Francesca. But determined, intelligent and precocious. Sean was obscenely confident and relaxed.

"Are you looking at me to see if you can see your father in me?" he asked Jack.

"Yes. Yes, I am." Jack unbuttoned his coat and stood up to take it off.

"I'm looking at you wondering what Alistair must look like," said Sean.

"You've never seen a picture?"

"I've never even heard his name more than twice until yesterday. I don't think a family album was on the cards." He briefly toyed with his lighter, then put it away.

"Man. I... don't know what to say."

"I don't really think there is anything much to say? He didn't exist to me, that's all. I simply didn't have a father. I have no idea if his name is even on the birth certificate; I really have no idea how these things work."

"I can show you a picture... if you want?"

"It's not a big deal."

"I have a family picture in my wallet."

"That's fairly unusual for a twenty-something professional, surely?"

"My mother forced me to carry it. It's usually kept in one of the compartments of the wallet. I mean, I don't use it as a prop or anything."

"I can just see girls in bars loving the sight of Ma and Pa grinning for the camera." Sean looked at Jack and asked if he was going to produce the picture.

"You actually want to see it?" asked Jack.

"Of course I do. I'm not afraid of it. I think it would be interesting." He smiled and finished off his drink. Jack still had over half a pint left.

"I'll tell you what, you find it, and I'll get some more drinks in. You're on the… lager, I see. Can I get you a proper drink?"

"You're accusing me of what exactly?" said Jack, smiling.

"Drinking beer that bloats you and dulls your reactions. I'll get you something else." He headed off to the bar, cutting a path through the pub. The barmaid was there to greet him. At this distance, Jack couldn't pick much out, but she obviously liked Sean. He realised Sean had been here a while before he had even arrived. There was that back-story he hadn't factored in. He then felt better about her looking at him in the way she was. It also explained the 'chatty' remark at the bar that had earlier thrown him a little. And now, she was laughing at a joke he'd made and turned to get two whiskys from the optics. It seemed to Jack like now would be a good time for Sean to ask for her number, if he was going to get one. But Sean handed over a ten-pound note, took the change, and walked back.

Jack got his wallet out of his pocket and found the small family picture, Jack to the right of his mother, who was between him and his father.

"Here," said Sean, putting the drinks down on the table. There wasn't much ice in them, and not much Coke either. "Doubles. I thought I'd get it rolling along a little."

"Thank you." Jack raised his glass and they chinked them together. Sean took a big sip and then leaned in to Jack. "So, let's have a look at this picture." For the first time since they'd met, he betrayed a little nervousness.

"Here it is," said Jack, handing it over to him. On the back was written a date, in his mother's handwriting. Jack had passed it over with the back facing Sean. Holding it for just a second, Sean then flipped it and took a long look, eyes veering to the left of the picture.

"So, there he is. Dad. So to speak." Sean was deep in concentration. "He's... you look alike," he said, looking up at Jack. "I can understand why Mum might have... if she was wigging out. Which she was; I mean, really, I don't think she's well. Very unwell, in fact." He carried on staring at the picture. After around a minute or so, he reached out instinctively for his drink, taking it roughly and knocking back around half of it. He placed it down on the table, then looked up at Jack again.

"I know we're not really brothers in the sense of the word that most people would use and understand," Sean said. "But I'm an only child. I accepted it would remain this way with Mum getting to that certain age without any special someone in her life. Though I always kind of wanted a brother."

Jack didn't reply straight away, but held Sean's gaze. "I think that I did too," he replied. "I've always wondered why Mum and Dad didn't have any more children."

"Maybe we should, like, hug or something?"

"I don't know," said Jack, stiffening, not wanting to embrace this stranger in a pub.

"I'm *kidding*, Jack. You take yourself too seriously, dude,"

Sean said, finishing off the whisky with another brisk gulp. He looked at Jack with piercing eyes. "How about you finish off your drink and let's go somewhere a bit more lively."

"Right," said Jack, looking at his quarter of a pint and relatively untouched double.

"*Drinks*, I meant. Plural. I'm going to take this picture out and look at it over a cigarette. Be ready to leave when I get back." As he passed Jack, he put his left hand on Jack's shoulder. "We can always talk later. We should just use today to... meet each other." He left, the swing doors of the snug closing and moving on their hinges after he'd gone.

Jack finished the rest of his pint and placed it down on the table. His mind was racing. Moving on to the whisky and coke, he looked around at the people in the pub. They were carrying their conversations and sipping their pints. Occasionally, the volume was raised by a joke, or an anecdote. There was no big screen. The old man in this particular snug was slowly making his way through a crossword. Jack took a big gulp and left the rest of the drink, heading outside to join Sean, who he found leaning against the walk in the approaching evening dark, staring intently at a small, wallet-sized picture.

3

Jack's mouth felt dry and his head pounded as he turned towards the alarm clock. It rang out just as his eyes managed to focus on it. 7am: time to get up and head into the shower. He hadn't yet booked his time off and didn't really know what to do anymore. Last night's drinks with Sean had turned into a long session, moving from bar to bar, drink to drink. He tried to keep up with Sean and just about managed, his own extroversion slowly being uncovered from the sub-merged state it was in. Memories of Fran in bed with him faded away. This was the healing of time and distraction, of new pathways being forged in the mind, power-ways being rerouted all around the brain. Sean had asked him what he was up to tonight. He'd said that he was going to book time off then catch a train.

Sean had responded with a frown. "I'm only in town for a couple more nights. I'm back at work on Tuesday. Come out drinking with me." The music filled out the space, a bass line thumping a repeated motif.

"I... had planned to head out of town. For a fair while, in fact. I've packed a lot of stuff. It's ready to go."

Sean shook his head in an exaggerated way, the drink finally hitting him. The noise of a Soho bar cascaded around them. "You can't just run away from this, from *this*," he said, waving his hands to point at the bar. "Where are you going to go, man? What do you plan to *do*?"

"I don't know. I don't really plan to do anything."

Sean put his hands on Jack's shoulders and looked him in the eye. "You'll be as hungover as fuck tomorrow, but go to work, book your time off, and then meet me here at half-four, okay?"

"Half-four?"

"I need to take Mum to the doctor's. I'll be done by the afternoon. We need to talk this through. At least, you need to talk it through with me. Talk it through with someone who's now involved." The music grew louder as things started to blur at the edges. Jack lost his train of thought for a moment, and then things fell into focus.

"I'll see you tomorrow, then."

"I'm out of here, dude." Sean stood up, knocked a cigarette out of his packet and put his into his mouth. Grabbing his jacket, he turned to Jack and indicated that he was going outside for a cigarette. "Go home, Jack, you're pissed. I'll make my own way back."

"Surely you're getting the Tube, too?"

Sean got his phone out. "I've got some people to catch up with just down the road. Tomorrow, okay?" Sean left, not looking back, his outline disappearing into a crowd of people.

The morning light hurt Jack's eyes. The shower gave him temporary relief, the hot, scalding water just about waking him up. As he sat, po-faced in a dressing gown, staring at his flight case, the clock ticking was the sound he heard above the creaking floorboards and rattling plumbing. Anne's door clunked shut as she skipped into the shower with light, quick steps. He thought about her naked. He pushed the idea out of his mind.

"I've got to get dressed," he said, out-loud, hands moving

to the belt of his robe. Downstairs, the postman posted something through the letterbox and it landed on the mat with a thump. Jack got up and moved to the wardrobe, opening it and getting out a shirt that he'd had dry-cleaned. It smelt crisp and fresh; it would last about ten minutes with the amount of booze he'd had yesterday. So he was meeting Sean at half-four? It would have to be half-five – he'd need to work the whole of today at least.

He went over to the phone dressed in just his shirt. 'Sean, change of plan, half-five, same place, see you there,' he wrote. It sent and he finished getting dressed. The journey to work was going to be extremely difficult while feeling this bad.

At work, he sat down in his chair after hanging up his jacket, and pulled his post-it notes closer. He jotted down the dates he wanted off and mentally prepared a little dialogue. Walking over to his boss's office, he knocked, entered, and explained his predicament, using his pre-planned story. There was a pause that he guessed was supposed to engender respect.

"That's a fair while off, Jack. And at quite short notice." His boss interlocked the fingers of his hands and let them rest in front of him.

"Well, it's either that, or I resign, Tom. Your choice." Jack stood tall above him; he hadn't sat down. The line manager considered the leverage that having someone as well-connected as Jack's father, Alistair, gave him there. Then considered the fall out of a resignation, especially Jack.

"Three weeks it is, then. Though you'll be falling quite far behind, young man."

"I'll make it up fairly quickly. I'm just… not in condition to carry out my duties at the moment, and I'd rather take the holiday option than the sick leave option. I'm sure that chimes with how you'd view it?"

Jack hated this man, with his delusions of grandeur. He didn't really hold that much power, but he thought that being responsible for signing off a few items made him extremely important. It didn't – not least to Jack, who just needed to finish his training and with his father's help could do it at one of several places.

"Here's the form. I've filled it out. You just need to sign it."

"Ah." Tom pulled the form across the desk from where Jack had set it down. He still hadn't taken a seat. Tom looked at it, signed where he was supposed to, then exhaled deeply. Jack felt the need to leave the office. He picked up the form.

"I'll email a copy of it to you, as per. I'll see you soon."

He closed the door on his way out, sat down at his desk and started his computer up, glancing over at the renewed pile of work in his in-tray. Someone walked up to his desk – it was one of the girls from across the office.

"Hi, Jack. I'm just heading down to get a coffee. Want to come? Should I get you anything?" she asked. She was wearing transparent lip-gloss and some citrus perfume, her brown work suit neatly cut around a medium-sized figure. Her patent leather shoes drew his eyes to them.

"I'll… come with you," he said, standing up and leaving the PC at the log-in screen. "I think a strong coffee might help kick start the day."

"Yep. I've got a big list from the other side so you can help me carry some of them. Good job I asked," she said, brushing against his shoulder after he'd put his coat on and they were walking towards the lifts. "Are you okay? You seem a little distracted."

"I'm just – intensely hungover."

"Know the feeling," she said, flicking some hair back over

her shoulder and jabbing the call button on the lift once they'd reached the lobby. He couldn't work out if she was flirting with him and really didn't care.

Five-thirty came quickly. Sean appeared at the entrance to the bar that they'd agreed to meet at, dressed in the same jacket but with dark blue denims and some brown leather loafers.

"I found these in a sale," he said, pointing down at his shoes.

"That's nice, Sean. They look – fine."

"I guess you'd spend a bit more, huh? Let's go inside," Sean said, walking past Jack and heading into the bar, where the music hadn't yet been turned up as high as it would go. Some tea-lights flickered at the tables, and, as they sat down, a waitress came over.

"Would you like a drink?" she said, her accent a little vague but European.

"I'd like a Chivas Regal and some Diet Coke," said Sean. "My... friend here would like –"

"I'd like a Corona, please," Jack added. She went away to get the drinks. The music was house, a simple chord sequence and a four-four beat ticking along like a metronome. Jack found himself tapping a finger out to it.

"I'm not sure what to call you really, Jack," said Sean, resuming. "I mean, should I have said, 'my brother'? Are you tapping your finger like an old man?"

"I have no idea, Sean. I really don't. And yes, I *am* tapping my finger. Why are you so hostile all the time?"

"It's the small town aggression, I'm sorry. Look, did you book your time off?"

"I got three weeks, which is the maximum before I have to get special dispensation."

"So?"

"So now? I was thinking of getting away, maybe renting a car, driving around. I need some space, I reckon. Some time to think things through. That was generally the plan." Jack leant back into the seat, making it creak slightly on its legs.

"You want to try and run away from the trouble?"

"I don't know if I'd put it quite like that, Sean."

"How else would you put it, then?"

"I want to get away. I want to get some perspective."

"On what?" Sean asked. "On my Mum, on this, on yourself, on your father?"

"On all of that, yes," said Jack, looking Sean in the eye and raising his volume slightly. "I want to try and get away from how I feel at the moment, too."

"You want to run away, then? And leave everyone else to cope? We're back to the same thing."

"This is not running away, Sean. I fully intend to come back. To my house, to my job. "

"By which time, you're hoping that Mum and I will be gone back from where we came from, and your Dad and Mum will have patched things up?"

"No…"

"Yes, you do. Admit it."

"Okay, okay. Something along those lines, yes."

"Good. Now we get to it."

The waitress came over and set Sean's drink down on a coaster that she took from a pile in the centre of the table, housed in a chrome-plated wire tower. She gave Jack his Corona and smiled at him. "Will there be anything else?" she said, blue eyes insistently set on Jack.

"No, that's fine, thanks. I'll wave if we do."

"No worries," she said, walking off, slowly.

"It must be your aftershave." He raised his drink. "Cheers," he said, clinking his glass to Jack's bottle and taking a measured sip. Jack took a swig from his beer, his throat dry and a little sore.

"That's better," said Jack. "That drinking last night made me feel like shit."

"It was a pretty big session. I didn't get to bed until three."

"I guess once you're past a certain point, you might as well," said Jack, his hands still around the neck of his beer. He dug at the painted-on labelling with his nail.

"I'm fairly used to it," said Sean. "It becomes routine. I took Mum to the walk-in clinic, and they said that she was suffering from some kind of shock or mental trauma. They gave her a prescription to calm her down and referred her to a specialist. Another prescription, as it turns out. She's been on antidepressants for some time." He paused to take another sip of his drink. It rattled with the amount of ice in it. He frowned, took some out and placed it in a glass someone had left on a nearby table. "Actually, I took one of her Valium, so I'm not in as much pain as you might think."

Jack didn't say anything.

"I don't think she was acting in her right mind, Jack. I don't really know how that makes you feel but, in any case, I'll be taking her back home tomorrow, or the day after, and I'll probably have to take some time off work too. I was thinking I might just jack it in; I mean, it's a retail job and I can get another one."

"Right," said Jack, still looking at the table. Someone had split candle wax onto the varnish.

"Jack," said Sean. Jack looked up. "You need to talk to me about this."

"Talk to you about *what*?"

"Why you're running away, even if its only for three weeks. You need to understand that you can't run away from yourself, dude. You just can't."

"I would think that's fairly self-evident."

"Is it? Then why is an intelligent young man like yourself thinking about doing the self same thing while bleating about it in a bar? What, because you're *special*? Because you alone could do it with your amazing force of will?"

"What are you talking about, Sean? You're making no sense."

"You'll get to where, Jack? The end of the motorway, to a hotel, to a shag after a bad night out in a provincial town? Where is that going to take you? Is this *On The Road* for the rental car driver?"

"You're sounding like a prick, Sean. I don't understand why you would know more about this than I would? Why your theories and dictums hold credence where mine don't?"

"I just know about running away. I would think that with Mum and her head buried in the sand for decades, and her insistence on moving, on thinking about something else, I think… that I would know."

"You're saying that what she ran away from came out in the end?"

"Running away didn't do shit, Jack. You are always delaying the inevitable confrontation. Do you know how many times I moved as a kid? Once I was old enough to be put into childcare during the day, she was a nomad. I went from staying with my grandmother while Mum was working to being shunted around while she moved from place to place, trying harder and harder to become someone that wasn't her. I know about this stuff because it left me with a sense of vacuity that I still can't shake." Sean paused and fidgeted in his pocket. He got his lighter and cigarettes out and put them on the table, next to the tea-light that was flickering from a draft made by the fan on the ceiling. Switched onto a low setting, it turned around in lazy circles.

"I'm going outside for a cigarette, Jack. I'll be back soon."
For the first time he sounded upset and side-tracked by
unwanted memories brought back to the surface.
Conversations like this, Jack thought, were like stirring a
deep and clear puddle with a big stick. The girl behind the bar
gave him a glance from across the room. He smiled, briefly,
then sunk down into the chair and grabbed his beer.

Sean came back in after five minutes or so.

"Do you want me to come with you, Jack? So that I can
witness the inoperancy of running away at first hand? So that
I can take notes and give them to you when you get home?"

"Are you being serious?"

"I can leave my job. Mum will be fine if I take her back to
Gran's. It's probably where she should go anyway. I'm hardly
prime carer material. I'd make things worse."

"I'll say."

"That wasn't meant as an opening for you, Jack."

"Sorry."

"Yes," said Sean, shifting in his seat and reaching out for
his drink. "I just want you to know that you can try to clear
your head by moving, by running, by picking up speed and
abandoning locations, but you have to confront yourself.
That's what I want you to know, Jack." Sean looked at Jack
with a half-smile playing on his lips, his face set in a semi-
serious expression.

"Come with me then," said Jack.

4

A few days later, Jack came out of the car hire shop with some keys, throwing them at Sean on the forecourt.

"That red Lotus over there," he said. "You can take it up to the M25."

He'd unlocked it at the remote and wheeled his flight case up to it, opening the boot. He put the case in and Sean hoisted in a rucksack. The boot shut with a satisfying clunk. The day was cold but sunny, the air fresh and crisp.

"On second thoughts," said Sean, "this is your escapist fantasy. You can take the keys." He threw back them across at Jack, who had to move slightly to his right to catch them.

"Not a keen sportsman, then?"

"Fuck off," Sean said, a smile on his face as they walked past each other near the front bonnet. Jack got in, revelling in the leather seats and wooden dash. Sean closed his door heavily. With the key in, Jack turned the engine over and it started with a roar.

"This one is supposed to be the 'beast of the pack', according the guy behind the desk."

"Couldn't you have got an Escalade or something? How am I going to bang girls in this little thing?" He looked across at Jack.

Jack said nothing, trying the biting point and then slipping the car into first, the bonnet rising slightly as the drive plates met. He then backed off the biting point and checked his phone before placing it back into his pocket.

"Can I smoke in here?" asked Sean.

"No, they're all non-smoking. I did check. You'll have to wait until we get there," he said, the tyres squealing as Jack put the car into a forty-five degree turn at speed out of the forecourt and onto the road. It was clear for a few hundred metres, the roads quiet in the mid-afternoon. He over revved it and slipped into second, moving up through the gears as the car picked up pace. In fourth too soon, he pushed down the gas pedal and dropped into third, the acceleration pushing Sean back into his passenger seat. Jack pointed the nose at the slip road onto the dual carriageway and brought the car up to forty-miles-an-hour.

"Put your seatbelt on, Sean," said Jack, who then said nothing until they were on the motorway, the car smelling of Sean's mints and the Forest Fresh stick dangling from the rear-view mirror. Between lunchtime and rush hour, the car ate up the distance to the motorway. Jack took it onto the M25. He wanted to swing it out from orbit.

They came, eventually, to various locations. Car parks in hotels, bars and clubs, in towns with similar signs but changing accents. The Lotus ran smoothly between destinations. Sean looked over at Jack on occasions to see a man fixed on the next mile countdown and turn off, on hitting the next exit to get to where they were going. His battered leather-bound road atlas was laid on Sean's lap as he directed him to an A-road, a B-road. A road with no letter before it. What Jack was after wasn't clear. Small medieval towns with their roads in a maze, a Roman bath that they sat in, wordlessly. They had an ice cream along a promenade. Jack found delight in trying to skim pebbles across the water of a lake.

They visited the Beach House, Jack calling Ray for the address. They stood in the front garden, the house sold to new occupants and unable to get any closer. Four beers into a night with a football match on a widescreen television, the sea breeze blew in through the open patio doors on two half-brothers starting to find a bond. Sean drove for a while; he stopped at petrol stations to buy cigarettes and mints, throwing a can of Diet Coke at Jack as he switched the car from gear to gear.

Jack felt Fran slip away even as she was closer to him by degrees, through her son. He felt the pathways of memory dust over; the concrete cracked as it weathered in the frost and the ice. The rain and the sleet came in patches as they drove, wipers on full, the road a reflective mirror. Jack couldn't see himself in the rain-dazzle. Red lights swirled as he got lost in a memory of impossible desire. He couldn't capture it in any tangible way – it had to exist silently and without a form in some compartment of the past that he knew he'd never want to visit again.

Jack was running from himself, towards distant lands, towards the sea and away from what had come before. The fourth morning into the second week, he got up, mouth dry, as Sean lay asleep on the futon across the room. Sean stirred too as the light came streaming through the window. They'd forgotten to draw the curtains as they'd stumbled in the night before. He reached out instinctively for his cigarettes, but they were on the dresser. His hand came back grasping air.

Jack sat up, and pushed the bed sheets back. He stepped over to Sean and knelt down to bring himself face to face with him. Sean had three-day old stubble, his eyes just about open for business.

"Sean, I think you were right."

"Right... about what?" he said, stretching his legs and yawning.

"Nothing has changed, has it? Nothing has changed."

"You can't run from yourself, dude. I told you. You can only run."

"Let's go back."

5

They drove back the next day, after time spent sitting sullenly in deckchairs on a blustery beach. The sand got everywhere and slowly the heat of the sun dissipated. Sean put his finished cigarettes in an ash pouch that he'd been given, so that he wasn't dropping butts on coastal beauty spots. Jack hummed a tune he remembered from the mid-nineties. Something about catching a train. The sky was partly cloudy, disparate and ragged.

"Ready?"

"Soon as I get the sand out of my socks, dude."

"Let's go then."

They walked up to the car. Sean had to turn his socks inside out. Eventually, he got his rucksack out of the boot and changed the pair he had on, deciding to slip on his loafers for the journey. Jack's flight case had a big dent from where they'd rolled it down a hill.

The engine fired up smoothly and Jack knew how to handle the car now, its nuances and needs. It was hungry for petrol. He drove it all the way back to London, only taking breaks to go to the toilet, fill up, or grab a bad cup of coffee from the overpriced service stations along the way.

Eventually, he tired of stopping, just racing down the fast lane, occasionally flashing his headlights at someone to get out of the way. A BMW driver tried to race him part of the way. Jack had slowed down, indicating clearly that he didn't really want to push past 100. Gesturing idiotically, the BMW driver shot ahead. Jack whacked the pedal down and gunned past it, undertaking in the middle lane and stripping away from it as fast he could. He made out the blank face of the other driver in his rearview mirror, disappearing quickly. He felt nothing.

The motorway was periodically empty as dusk fell. The lights got brighter as the sun went down. The traffic built up as he got to London, the distances between cars getting shorter, tempers flaring as the density of traffic overwhelmed the road. They crawled the last bit of the journey before Jack lost patience and hauled the car off the motorway, making his way at speed along the A-roads, sighing as bad drivers cut him up or didn't signal.

All the way, he'd been playing music. The mood in the car would change on a whim as 'Stripped' gave way to 'Wire' which gave way to 'Let Down'. Some guitar. A chord change from the 90s. His indie scene jeans and Marlboro Lights. The beer spillage and ruined shoes. At one point, Jack swerved tightly around a desolate suburban roundabout with Bryan Ferry shuffling out of the speakers.

"This music is not right for this setting," said Sean, finally, waking from a long nap and wanting a cigarette. He yawned and rolled his shoulders.

"We're nearly there. You've slept a while."

"Can't we put an album on?"

Jack paused to take a right back onto a dual carriageway, bringing the car back up to a decent speed. "Which one?"

"I don't know. Swerving around roundabouts in a rented car trying to outrun your mundane problems. How about 'Gold Against The Soul'?"

"Because your morning always feels too stale to justify?"

"That's the one. Stale as a two-week loaf."

"Go on then."

They had the Manic Street Preachers on for the rest of the journey, 'Gold Against The Soul' cueing as they raced from the lights past some youngsters in a decked out Ford Fiesta. Its tinted windows and wheel rims hadn't given it a new engine. '*Rock and roll has a conscience*' they sang as they sped past some place, sameness in the bricks and pavements. Finally, Jack pulled up outside his house.

"I haven't really thought this through." He stopped the engine.

"I guess you could sleep on my floor or on the couch, and catch the train back tomorrow?" He turned a little in his seat to look at Sean.

"I think Mum still has a couple of weeks to run on the lease of the flat, but I'm happy to stay here for the night."

"I'm too tired to drive you round there." Jack looked at his watch. It was a Longines. It was early enough for Sean to catch the Tube, but much easier for him to stay.

"The car has until the end of the week to run. I can drive you home tomorrow."

"It's no problem to catch the train."

"I want to… say hello to Fran," Jack said.

"You didn't clear your head then?" Sean smiled, but then looked out of the windscreen at nothing in particular as the silence stretched out.

"I think I did. And you were right about confronting the problems. I just have to check she's all right, you know? And then I'll say goodbye; get back on with things. I also have to go and check what's happening with my folks."

"Let's talk about this in the morning, man."

They got out of the car and grabbed their things from the

boot, Jack reaching into his pocket to get out his keys. The door opened as he reached for the lock; Anne looked out at them both.

"I saw you through the window, Jack. Welcome home stranger." She gave him a little hug. "Who is this?" she said, smiling at Sean.

"My half-brother." Anne's face suddenly displayed a sense of confusion Jack hadn't seen in a while and had missed. "I'll explain in a minute, let's go inside."

She turned and they followed with cases. Jack left his in the hall and Sean sauntered past him, putting his rucksack down in the living room. It backed onto the large kitchen, where Anne had put the kettle on and Jack followed her into.

"I didn't know you had a brother, Jack?" she asked, as Jack came in and sat down heavily, limbs aching from the exertion of driving hundreds of miles. Jack looked up at her with eyes beseeching distance and privacy. He wasn't up to fencing with Anne and hadn't wanted anyone to be up, or around. He changed the subject.

"Where are Gurj and Dylan?"

"They went out on a lad's night, apparently. Both single now."

"They went out to the *same* place? Amazing. You go away for a bit, look what happens. The urban music scene changes entirely."

Sean stood up and walked into the kitchen. It had recently been cleaned, the surfaces wiped down. The stove-top coffee maker had been put away, much to Jack's momentary consternation.

"Jack, you didn't tell me you lived with such a delightful creature," Sean said, turning to look at Anne and then joining her, resting against the worktop. "Or did you want to keep her to yourself?" Anne laughed nervously.

"Sean, I thought you were tired? There's a sleeping bag under my bed."

"Jack, don't be a grump," said Anne. "Maybe I should pour us all a drink instead? Wine?" She practically existed on the calories in Blossom Hill since starting to teach and there was always some in the fridge.

"Are you sure you can spare it, Anne?" teased Jack, having moved to the couch in the lounge, already looking sleepy.

"Jack," she said, playfully. She grabbed two wine glasses in addition to her own and set them out on the worktop, just as the kettle boiled.

"I think Jack could use a cup of coffee, first, eh?" said Sean, looking over at him.

"Agreed," he said from the other room.

"Shall I make it?" Sean asked Anne.

"No, I'll get it. Why don't you go and sit down?"

"Sure," Sean said. "So… can I smoke in here?"

"Yes," said Jack. "But she'll hate you for it."

"I'm fine with it!" Anne insisted. Her words were just a little slurred, enough for Jack to pick up on.

"She fancies you, Sean."

"Shut up, Jack," Anne said. Her mood changed suddenly. "Just stop it."

Jack was sleepy and unguarded after too many hours on the road. "And she'll fancy you more after that big glass of wine she's pouring."

Anne snapped, already brittle. "You're such a bastard, Jack." She slammed the wine bottle down. "I wish you hadn't come back now. I was looking forward to you coming through that door but you're so selfish," she said, tears suddenly in her eyes. She slid the wine bottle across the worktop towards the wall and stormed past them, heading upstairs, her feet oddly heavy and uncoordinated on the stairs. So she'd definitely had a glass or two already, Jack surmised. Maybe another bottle even? Some of those big, outsize wine stems sold in upmarket department stores. His brain was fuzzed with cynicism and tiredness.

"That was a shit thing to do," said Sean.

"What?" Jack looked over at Sean and shrugged his shoulders.

"I can tell from the moment I met her that she fancies you. And what, are you jealous that she was nice to me?" The room was quiet. Jack was silent.

"You were a total shit, actually. She bounds out of the house to give you a big welcome back, probably thinking that a few weeks away has altered your perspective. Am I right? I'm guessing you might have had a thing, or maybe just a snog. Right?"

"Sean, why are you always... so fucking incisive, huh? Just... stop."

"I'm sleeping down here tonight, Jack. On that very comfy couch you're on. Don't worry about the sleeping bag. So go up stairs and say sorry."

"Since when were you the diplomat? You're always saying stuff out-loud that makes what I just said look like tea party chit-chat."

"It's about *context*, Jack. It's about not taking out a shitty drive on a beautiful girl who rushes out to say hello to you."

"Yes, well. I don't know." Jack looked over at Sean. "You're going to call it a night then?"

"You look pretty tired, bro'. I'd guess we're at the end of today's battery charge."

He'd not used that epithet for Jack before. Jack paused, about to say something. But it was a moment that he didn't want to blunder into, with some badly chosen words that stuck in the throat, half-bitten crisp fragments you couldn't cough up or swallow. He sleepily got up and patted Sean on his shoulder.

"I'll see you tomorrow, Sean."

Jack trudged up the stairs. He walked past Anne's door on the way to the bathroom, then turned back and knocked. He heard a "go away" but he pushed it open, to find her on the bed, face angled away from the door and towards the wall.

"I'm sorry, Anne. I've had a really tiring drive and I wasn't thinking."

"Jack, you already know how I feel. You've known for months how I've felt. You knew that what you just said would hurt me," she said, her voice cracking on the syllables.

"I... will keep my distance."

"I don't want you to be distant, Jack. I want you to be mine." Her voice was suffused with the effects of an evening alone drinking wine. Jack had pulled up at the house and pulled into an altercation that was always going to happen.

"I like you a lot Anne. I do. I've not really said anything about it. But my head is in entirely the wrong place at the moment. And it's not fair on you."

"Go away, Jack. Just go away." She was lying on the bed, face into the pillow.

He stood there for a few seconds, then quietly pulled the door shut, and headed to the bathroom, regretfully brushing his teeth and very slowly heading downstairs to get a glass of water.

6

Jack drove Sean home the next day. They made an early start, eating some toast and having a coffee in silence. Sean went up to the bathroom and shaved using one of Jack's disposables. When clean shaven, the resemblance between them both was a little clearer. He had Fran's eyes, soulful and intelligent.

Jack switched on the radio in the kitchen as he put the dishes into the dishwasher. Anne came down as they left. Sean headed off to wait in the car, nodding almost imperceptibly at Jack as he passed. Jack came back in, tired. Anne looked as if she had a painful hangover. She was searching distractedly for her mug. She turned around when she heard Jack step into the kitchen.

"I'm sorry about last night, Anne."

"Yeah? That's good," she said, looking down at the floor.

"I don't want to play with your feelings. I'm going to keep my distance. I can't move out right now, but if it makes it easier on you, then I will try to move out soon. If it has come to that. I could always stay with my Mum, being as... well, my parents have split up."

"Oh, I didn't..."

"We've not spoken much, I know. I don't know about much anymore. I'm just taking it all very slowly."

"Right," she said, looking pale.

"Can I get you a glass of water or something? You look pretty drained."

"I'm fine. I just need to find my mug."

"I think it might be in the other cupboard with the tumblers, I was taking the clean stuff out of the dishwasher just now." She moved, just slightly, but stopped once more.

"I'm going to throw up, Jack," she said, and turned, vomiting into the sink. She retched a few times, and stayed facing into the sink.

"Anne?" She didn't rise from the sink. He couldn't imagine her wanting to be seen in this state. "Do you want me to –"

"Just go, Jack. Please."

He turned and left.

As he climbed into the driver's seat, Sean asked him how it went.

"Well, she mumbled a few words, turned around, and puked into the sink."

"Possibly, a harsh indictment of what she thought of your shit, Jack." He lit his cigarette and wound down the window. "Or maybe she was hammered last night and you could have called her a slut and it would have made no difference? I'm not always right."

Jack looked across at him, frowning, and then started the car up, gently edging it out of the parked cars on the road. He fired it up, crossing the white lines, rounding the corners, jerking to a stop. A brakepad goes down. The wind whipping on the windscreen. A light rain falls, the wipers on. Jack switched on the seat heaters at one point but Sean complained that he felt like he'd wet himself. He kept up the pace until they reached Sean's house. Conversation was brief and held over the stereo, mainly Flaming Lips, or during the pauses between songs.

Fran's house was a two-bedroom property with a large garden, attractive and red brick. There was a neatly trimmed hedge in the front garden. Sash windows made up the look.

"Do you know if she's home?" asked Jack.

"She just got back from my Gran's house. I... really don't know if it's a good idea for you two to see each other." Sean unbuckled his seatbelt, which whirred into the door frame. He absentmindedly got a stick of chewing gum out from his jacket pocket and undid the wrapping.

"I think that I should see her. I think I want her to see us together."

"She's not... going to see it as her two sons re-united, in case that's your tack."

"What?" snapped Jack. "No, of course not."

"Jack, lighten up. You worry too much about semantics. Fine, come in – I'll make you a brew."

Sean got out and headed to the boot, slinging his rucksack around his right shoulder.

"The garden's really nice. You'll like it," Sean said as they walked up the pathway, the paving stones all neatly kept. Jack looked back at the red Lotus in the driveway. He turned to look forward, seeing a gloss black doorway with brass numbers on it and a large knocker. His family house flashed into his mind: the imposing doorway, Alistair at the door, eyes slanted in disapproval at his son, who was swaying from left to right and clutching a plastic tray, grease stains on his shirt-cuffs.

"It's late," he'd say.

"Yeah, past *your* bed-time, for sure," Jack would reply, stumbling into the kitchen to get another drink and maybe fall asleep on the granite worktop. His mother would come down in the night and nudge him awake, leading him to his bed. He loved his mother. His father had always been a mystery to him. It was like that, with sons and their fascination. It was their Pyrrhic desire to understand their own creation.

Fran was home. She came to the door as Sean opened it with his key. She stared at Jack.

"So, I gather you've been driving around the country with my son?"

"Yes."

"I'm surprised he didn't wear you out," she said. She smiled, but it was a different smile to the one before. It was slower and less radiant. It looked drugged and unfocused. "Let's not stand in the hallway like this anyway. Do you want to come in?" It wasn't an invitation, more a question that he had to answer.

"Yes, I'd like to."

"Can we dispense with this and let me put my pack down?" muttered Sean, heading off into the lounge.

Fran walked into the large, well-lit kitchen. There was a big dining table strewn with newspapers.

"I'll make you a coffee, Jack. Then I think you should go. I don't really feel much like conversation"

"That's fine," he said, his word clipped and short.

"Why did you come here?"

"To drop Sean off?" Jack looked down at his fingers. From a back room, some music played.

"You could have put him on a train? I bet he suggested it."

"Yes, he did." Jack put his hands into his pockets. "Are you feeling better?"

"Better? Than before? Yes, I am."

She turned to the coffee machine and he felt a pull to the past. It was hazy and indistinct.

"You caused a lot of heartache, Fran."

"Did you come here to tell me this in person, Jack? I'm not amused." Sean walked into the kitchen just as she spoke, cutting her off. "Are we going to do this like adults?" he said.

"Didn't we lose our chance to do that, Sean?" said Jack. "When this whole thing kicked off?" He was angry at Fran's anger. The situation was feeding on the emotions in the room.

"Jack, play nice," said Sean, looking at him, impassively. He sat down at the dining table and asked Fran, "Could you make a coffee for me too, please?"

Jack sat down, too, taking a deep breath. Fran set the coffee machine to make three espressos, which it did fairly rapidly. She poured them out into little espresso cups and brought them over with a bowl of sugar, all on a black tray.

"Thanks," said Sean.

"Fran, I only came here just to see if you were okay and that you were back on track. If you are, I'm happy, and I'm going to head back to London."

"I'm on the mend," she said. "Do you want any biscuits? Any *biscotti*?" Her mood seem to be veering from one place to another. There was a wild look in her eye. He felt a little afraid of what she might say next.

"No," said Jack. He took a sip of espresso. The blend was aromatic and deep.

"This is nice, thank you." He took another sip. "It's also been good to meet Sean. He's... a credit to you." Sean looked at his, creasing his brow. "I can't believe he came from Dad."

The remark was at the point of being risqué, but Fran looked back at Jack and saw something that she'd never noticed in Alistair. Jack had deeper understanding. Alistair had snatched at conclusions and forced his thoughts onto a framework he himself had constructed.

"I think my folks are separating," Jack said, without any real tone in his voice. "Or at least, Dad has moved out. I think he might even be staying with Ray. Ray's left his house too. I'm not sure what's happening to be honest. I've not spoken to them. It might work itself out." He stopped talking and finished what was left in his coffee cup. There was a long silence. Outside, they heard the rain start up against the window panes. It came in light at first; then, after a minute or so, it drove down onto the house in big sheets.

"Sean, I'm going home," Jack said. He held out his hand, and they both stood up. They shook hands, and then hugged each other. Fran looked on, a little surprised.

"I'll see you soon, bro'," said Sean.

"For sure," said Jack, turning to go. He stopped, and turned back. The kitchen was sunlit and warm. It smelled of coffee and faintly of cigarettes. Sean was looking at him and then at his mother, his head turning slowly between them.

"Goodbye, Francesca," Jack said, with an air of finality.

"Goodbye, Jack," she said, her voice tired and slow, her gaze slipping to the floor as he walked out.

7

The ping of the elevator arriving meant the small crowd in the ground floor lobby started milling around, like sheep in a panic. The warm rush of a train into the platform was all it took to set the pack moving. Jack walked through them and up the stairs, his headphones piping music into his ears, interrupted only by the sound of his soles on the steps. He stopped at the fourth floor, switched off the music, and put the headphones away in his bag.

Work meant hanging up his coat, turning on his computer and sitting down on his chair. It meant sending emails and heading out to meet with clients. It meant the inane conversations in the kitchen, in the corridors, in the canteen, on the way to the pub. It meant someone eating an apple in the open plan. It meant waiting in the queues for the cash machine.

His hair was getting longer and he ran his fingers through it as the familiar start-up screen threatened to overwhelm any morning enthusiasm. Jean came over, on the coffee run. He got up, slipped his coat back on, and headed out with her, deferring the start of the day. She loved his two-day stubble and his tailored shirts. He liked that she wore lip-gloss to the office. He still couldn't tell if she was flirting with him and still didn't care.

You can never run away from yourself. You can never run

from who you are. You can cross the seas and change the skies, but you take your spirit with you. The spirit of your successes, your failures, your inadequacies, your strengths: it is your close companion, is always with you; it is your double shadow in the twin suns of your parentage.

As his was thinking, Jack tried to light a cigarette outside the building with a sheet of matches he'd picked up in a Shoreditch bar. They were flimsy and winter was setting in. A gust of wind blew the first one out. Cupping it, Jean stood to his side. He felt the match burn out and sting his fingers, the startling pain stirring a recognition. He shook the match off and it made its way to the floor in an arc. A puff of smoke clung to them both and then drifted off.

He left the cigarette clamped in his mouth, shaking his hand slightly, trying to ignore the pain.

"Did you get your finger, Jack?" asked Jean.

"A little. Let's keep walking."

The envelope kept popping up in his system tray, emails trickling in all day. He kept checking back on news websites at an improbable rate. The news stayed fairly static, a slow day. He walked to the floor below to get a new set of red and blue pens from the stationary cupboard.

The car that he'd driven with Sean was a memory now, parked up on some forecourt or being sped around by someone else. He recalled a day in the sun at a seaside town, walking along the seafront, a taste of salt in the air. He pictured an emphatic embrace from Fran one night, the two of them drunk and looking out at London through a half-open window. Half of what they saw was reflection; the two of them improbably intertwined. The mesh of her hair in his fingers was a sensation that was ebbing away from his life. There he was, knees bent, a shambles on a bathroom floor. He'd looked up and noticed a crack in the window, thought about the crack when she'd put the phone down on him. He thought about his father's slumped posture in their house as he spoke about her. He thought about the decades long lie that had broken his parent's marriage.

These were his fragments and here was his day. This was his kingdom, such as it was.

He paused a little before he switched the computer off for the day, the sun on the opposite side of the building now. His phone was in his jacket pocket. He left the building by the usual route, enjoying the first wave of fresh air on his face after the air-con office. The entrance to the Tube was busy. He was weightless there. There was no gravity to speak of, only the used wrappers, the repetition, and the endless creation of yet more narrative, yet more history. London is beautiful as the sun sets and the neon starts out, the dusk shading into evening. The evening shades into a night, a partaking in the daily rebirth and reinvention.

Jack was seeing Ray that night for a drink at the flat Ray was renting. Elizabeth went on long runs and they spoke on the phone, Ray laying on his side on a bed decked out in masculine colours. He had allowed himself a talking clock and a Goblin Teasmaid.

"I miss you," she had said, at long last.

"I think that we'll work it out," he had replied, looking vacantly at the chest of draws across the room, the top covered with his junk, piles of receipts and a money clip stuffed with twenty pound notes.

"How is the house?" he asked.

"Empty," she replied. "There are echoes in some of the rooms now. Now that all your junk is gone."

Ray laughed and turned onto his other side.

Jack sat in the kitchen as Ray poured them both a drink. He was sharing the two-bedroom flat with Alistair. His father's room was neat and tidy. He sat, moodily, in the corner armchair, reading his newspapers and hardback fiction. Rachel had asked for a divorce and had instructed solicitors. She had taken solace in friends. Dark rumours circulated.

Jack's phone whirred into action in his pocket. It was Sean. 'I will see you next weekend, then. Bring your party pants. SD.' Jack put the phone away as Ray started on another anecdote about a friend of his.

He couldn't believe that Ray had started wearing vests indoors.

Anne would meet him furtively in the park and they would link arms; he would walk her to the pub. There is a weight of memory we carry around with us. Jack hadn't pulled away from anything; he'd walked towards it. When in London, Sean would walk into his house with his shades on, and ask Jack if he could borrow his hair gel. Dylan was starting to get on his nerves.

Jack had managed to run away from nothing at all. It was here, in whatever made up Jack Wilson. The sky was golden oranges and honey as the sun slowly set. He watched Sean light a cigarette and thought about Ray and Alistair playing chess in the flat, Tori Amos's *Little Earthquakes* on the stereo. Alistair would reach to take his tie off and fold up his cuffs. Ray walked to the kitchen to get another beer in a designer vest. It was comical.

London is so beautiful at nine o'clock in the evening. The park was cold, the trees were huge silhouettes. Each scene a picture postcard; the repetition; the flash photography. The street air was brisk, mingled with the muggy warmth of the city at night. A thousand noises made up the background.

205

From wherever he was, he could see Canary Wharf. Cars passed by, the roar of traffic a dull rumble. Streetlamps made cones of yellow sodium light on the wet pavement. Anne held his hand tightly. He wanted something to take this doubt and cast it aside. He wanted something that he could run towards. He wanted something warm and welcoming to lead him home. He held out his hands. He was holding out his hands.